Water. Man's most precious commodity is a luxury of the past. Radioactive waste from years of industrial dumping has caused the sea to form a protective skin strong enough to devastate the Earth it once sustained.

And while the remorseless sun beats down on the dying land, civilization itself begins to crack. Violence erupts and insanity reigns as the remnants of mankind struggle for survival in a world-wide desert of despair.

J G BALLARD was born in 1930 in Shanghai, China, where his father was a businessman. His first short story appeared in *New Worlds* in 1956, and after working on scientific journals he published his first major novel, *The Drowned World*, in 1962. His acclaimed 1984 novel *Empire of the Sun* won the *Guardian* Fiction Prize and the James Tait Black Memorial Prize, and was shortlisted for the Booker Prize. It was later filmed by Steven Spielberg. J G Ballard's recent novels include *Rushing to Paradise*, *Cocaine Nights* and *Super-Cannes*, all of which are available from Flamingo.

By J G Ballard

flamingo sixties classic

J G Ballard

THE DROUGHT

Flamingo
An Imprint of HarperCollins*Publishers*

Flamingo
An imprint of HarperCollins*Publishers*
77–85 Fulham Palace Road,
Hammersmith, London w6 8jb

Flamingo is a registered trade mark of HarperCollins Publishers Ltd.

www.fireandwater.com

This Flamingo Sixties Classic edition published 2001
9 8 7 6 5 4 3 2 1

First published in Great Britain by Jonathan Cape Ltd 1965

ISBN 0 00 711518 0

Set in Monotype Apollo and Optima Display by
Rowland Phototypesetting Ltd
Bury St Edmunds, Suffolk

Printed and bound in Great Britain by
Clays Ltd, St Ives plc

Contents

v

Part One

1

The Draining Lake

At noon, when Dr Charles Ransom moored his houseboat in the entrance to the river, he saw Quilter, the idiot son of the old woman who lived in the ramshackle barge outside the yacht basin, standing on a spur of exposed rock on the opposite bank and smiling at the dead birds floating in the water below his feet. The reflection of his swollen head swam like a deformed nimbus among the limp plumage. The caking mud-bank was speckled with pieces of paper and driftwood, and to Ransom the dream-faced figure of Quilter resembled a demented faun strewing himself with leaves as he mourned for the lost spirit of the river.

Ransom secured the bow and stern lines to the jetty, deciding that the comparison was less than apt. Although Quilter spent as much time watching the river as Ransom and everyone else, his motives would be typically perverse. The continued fall of the river, sustained through the spring and summer drought, gave him a kind of warped pleasure, even if he and his mother had been the first to suffer. Their derelict barge – an eccentric gift from Quilter's protector, Richard Foster Lomax, the architect who was Ransom's neighbour – had now taken on a thirty-degree list, and a further fall of even a few inches in the level of the water would split its hull like a desiccated pumpkin.

Shielding his eyes from the sunlight, Ransom surveyed the silent banks of the river as they wound westwards to

3

the city of Mount Royal five miles away. For a week he had been out on the lake, sailing the houseboat among the draining creeks and mud-flats as he waited for the evacuation of the city to end. After the closure of the hospital at Mount Royal he intended to leave for the coast, but at the last moment decided to spend a few final days on the lake before it vanished for good. Now and then, between the humps of damp mud emerging from the centre of the lake, he had seen the distant span of the motor-bridge across the river, the windows of thousands of cars and trucks flashing like jewelled lances as they set off along the coast road for the south; but for most of the period he had been alone. Suspended like the houseboat above the dissolving glass of the water, time had seemed becalmed.

Ransom postponed his return until all movement along the bridge had ended. By then the lake, once a stretch of open water thirty miles in length, had subsided into a series of small pools and channels, separated by the banks of draining mud. A few last fishing craft sailed among them, their crews standing shoulder to shoulder in the bows. The drab-suited men from the settlement, thin faces hidden under their black caps, had gazed at Ransom's houseboat with the numbed expressions of a group of lost whaling men too exhausted by some private tragedy to rope in this stranded catch.

By contrast, the slow transformation of the lake exhilarated Ransom. As the wide sheets of water contracted, first into shallow lagoons and then into a maze of creeks, the wet dunes of the lake bed seemed to emerge from another dimension. On the last morning he woke to find the houseboat beached at the end of a small cove. The slopes of mud, covered with the bodies of dead birds and fish, stretched above him like the shores of a dream.

As he approached the entrance to the river, steering the houseboat among the stranded yachts and fishing boats, the lakeside town of Hamilton was deserted. Along the fishermen's quays the boat-houses were empty, and the white forms of the drying fish hung in the shadows from the lines of hooks. Refuse fires smouldered in the water-front gardens, their smoke drifting past the open windows that swung in the warm air. Nothing moved in the streets. Ransom had assumed that a few people would remain behind, waiting until the main exodus to the coast was over, but Quilter's presence, like his ambiguous smile, in some way was an obscure omen, one of the many irrational signs that had revealed the real progress of the drought during the confusion of the past months.

A hundred yards to his right, beyond the concrete pillars of the motor-bridge, the wooden piles of the fuel depot were visible above the cracked mud. The floating pier had touched bottom, and the fishing boats usually moored against it had moved off into the centre of the channel. Normally, in late summer, the river would have been three hundred feet wide, but it was now barely half this – a shallow creek winding its slow way along the flat gutter of the banks.

Next to the fuel depot was the yacht basin, with the Quilters' barge moored against its bows. After signing the vessel over to them at the depot, Lomax had added a single gallon of diesel oil in a quixotic gesture of generosity, barely enough fuel for the couple to navigate the fifty yards to the basin. Refused entry, they had taken up their mooring outside. Here Mrs Quilter sat all day on the hatch-way, her faded red hair blown around her black shawl, muttering at the people going down to the water's edge with their buckets.

Ransom could see her now, beaked nose flashing to left and right like an irritable parrot's as she flicked at her dark face with a Chinese fan, indifferent to the heat and the river's stench. She had been sitting in the same place when he set off in the houseboat, her ribald shouts egging on the week-end mariners laying a line of cement-filled bags across the entrance to the yacht basin. Even at flood barely enough water entered the harbour to irrigate its narrow docks, and this had now leaked back into the river, settling the smartly decked craft into their own mud. Deserted by their owners, the yachts were presided over by Mrs Quilter's witch-like presence.

Despite her grotesque appearance and insane son, Ransom admired this old woman of the barges. Often during the winter he crossed the rotting gangway into the gloomy interior of the barge, where she lay on a feather mattress tied to the chart table, wheezing to herself. The single cabin, filled with dusty lanterns, was a maze of filthy recesses veiled by old lace shawls. After filling her tea-pot from the flask of gin in his valise, Ransom would be rowed back across the river in her son's leaking coracle, Quilter's great eyes below the hydrocephalic forehead staring at him through the rain like wild moons.

Rain! — at the recollection of what the term had once meant, Ransom looked up at the sky. Unmasked by clouds or vapour, the sun hung over his head like an ever-attendant genie. The fields and roads adjoining the river were covered with the same unvarying light, a glazed yellow canopy that embalmed everything in its heat.

Below the jetty Ransom had staked a line of coloured poles into the water, but the rapid fall in the level needed little calculation. In the previous three months the river had dropped some twenty feet, shrinking to less than a quarter of its original volume. As it sank, it seemed to pull everything towards it. The banks were now opposing cliffs, topped by the inverted tents suspended from the chimneys of the riverside houses. Originally designed as rain-traps — though no rain had ever fallen into them — the canvas envelopes had been transformed into a line of aerial garbage scoops, the bowls of dust and leaves raised like offerings to the sun.

Ransom crossed the deck and stepped down into the steering well. He waved to Quilter, who was watching him with a drifting smile. Behind him, along the deserted wharfs, the bodies of the drying fish turned slowly in the air.

'Tell your mother to move the barge,' Ransom called across the interval of slack water. 'The river is still falling.'

Quilter ignored this. He pointed to the blurred forms moving slowly below the surface.

'Clouds,' he said.

'What?'

'Clouds,' Quilter repeated. 'Full of water, doctor.'

Ransom stepped through the hatchway into the cabin of the houseboat, smiling to himself at Quilter's bizarre humour. Despite his deformed skull and Caliban-like appearance, there was nothing stupid about Quilter. The dreamy, ironic smile, at times almost affectionate in its lingering glance, as if understanding Ransom's most intimate secrets, the seamed skull with its russet hair and the inverted planes of the face, in which the cheekbones were set back two or three inches, leaving deep hollows below the eyes – all these and a streak of unpredictable naivety made Quilter a daunting figure. Most people wisely left him alone, possibly because his invariable method of dealing with them was to pick unerringly on their weaknesses and work away at these like an inquisitor.

It was this instinct for failure, Ransom decided with wry amusement as Quilter watched him from his vantage point above the dead birds, that probably explained Quilter's persistent curiosity in his own case. For some time now Quilter had followed him around, no doubt assuming that Ransom's solitary week-ends among the marshes along the southern shore of the lake marked a reluctance to face up to certain failures in his life — principally, Ransom's estrangement from his wife Judith. However, Quilter's attempts to exploit this situation and provoke Ransom in various minor ways — by stealing the deck equipment from the houseboat, and disconnecting the power lines down the bank — had so far been unsuccessful in upsetting Ransom's tolerant good humour.

Quilter, of course, had been unable to grasp that the failure of Ransom's marriage was less a personal one than that of its urban context, in fact a failure of landscape, and that with his discovery of the river Ransom had at last found an environment in which he felt completely at home, a zone of identity in space and time. Quilter would have had little idea of the extent to which Ransom shared that sense of the community of the river, the unseen links between the people living on the margins of the channel, which for Ransom had begun to take the place of his marriage and his work at the hospital. All this had now been ended by the drought.

Throughout the long summer Ransom had watched the river shrinking, its countless associations fading as it narrowed into a shallow creek. Above all, Ransom was aware that the role of the river in time had changed. Once it had played the part of an immense fluid clock, the objects immersed in it taking up their positions like the stations of the sun and planets. The continued lateral movements of the river, its rise and fall and the varying pressures on the hull, were like the activity within a vast system of evolution, whose cumulative forward flow was as irrelevant and without meaning as the apparently linear motion of time itself. The real movements were those random and discontinuous relationships between the objects within it, those of himself and Mrs Quilter, her son and the dead birds and fish.

With the death of the river, so would vanish any contact

between those stranded on the drained floor. For the present the need to find some other measure of their relationships would be concealed by the problems of their own physical survival. None the less, Ransom was certain that the absence of this great moderator, which cast its bridges between all animate and inanimate objects alike, would prove of crucial importance. Each of them would soon literally be an island in an archipelago drained of time.

2

Mementoes

Helping himself to what was left of the whisky in the galley cabinet, Ransom sat down on the edge of the sink and began to scrape away the tar stains on his cotton trousers. Within the next hour he would have to go ashore, leaving the houseboat for the last time, but after a week on board he felt uneager to leave the craft and make all the social and mental readjustments necessary, minimal though these would now be. He had let his beard grow, and the rim of fair hair had been bleached almost white by the sunlight. This and his bare, sunburnt chest gave him the appearance of a seafaring Nordic anthropologist, standing with one hand on his mast, the other on his Malinowski. Although he gladly accepted this new persona, Ransom realized that it was still only notional, and that his real Odyssey lay before him, in the journey by land to the coast.

None the less, however much the role of single-handed yachtsman might be a pleasant masquerade, the houseboat seemed to have been his true home for longer than the few months he had owned it. He had seen the craft for sale the previous winter, while visiting a patient in the yacht basin, and bought it almost without thinking, on one of those gratuitous impulses he often used to let a fresh dimension into his life. To the surprise of the other yachtsmen, Ransom towed the craft away and moored it on the exposed bank below the motor-bridge. The mooring was a poor one at a nominal rent, the stench of the fish-quays drifting across the water, but the slip road near by gave him quick access to Hamilton and the hospital. The only hazards were the cigarette ends thrown down from the cars crossing the bridge. At night he would sit back in the steering well and watch the glowing parabolas extinguish themselves in the water around him.

Looking at the contents of the cabin as he sipped his drink, Ransom debated which of his possessions to take with him. The cabin had become, unintentionally, a repository of all the talismans of his life. On the bookself were the anatomy texts he had used in the dissecting room as a student, the pages stained with the formalin that leaked from the corpses on the tables, somewhere among them the unknown face of his surgeon father. On the desk by the stern window was the limestone paperweight he had cut from a chalk cliff as a child, the fossil shells embedded in its surface bearing a quantum of Jurassic time like a jewel. Behind it, the ark of his covenant, stood two photographs in a hinged blackwood frame. On the left was a snapshot of himself at the age of four, sitting on a lawn between his parents before their divorce. On the right, exorcizing this memory, was a faded reproduction of a small painting he had clipped from a magazine, 'Jours de Lenteur' by Yves Tanguy. With its smooth, pebble-like objects, drained of all associations, suspended on a washed tidal floor, this painting had helped to free him from the tiresome repetitions of everyday life. The rounded milky forms were isolated on their ocean bed like the houseboat on the exposed bank of the river.

Ransom picked up the frame and looked at the photograph of himself. Although he recognized the small, square-jawed face of the child on the lawn, there now seemed an absolute break of continuity between the two of them. The past had slipped away, leaving behind it, like the debris of a vanished glacier, a moraine of unrelated mementoes, the blunted nodes of the memories that now surrounded him in the houseboat. The craft was as much a capsule protecting him against the pressures and vacuums of time as the steel shell of an astronaut's vehicle guarded the pilot from the vagaries of space. Here his half-conscious memories of childhood and the past had been isolated and quantified, like the fragments of archaic minerals sealed behind glass cases in museums of geology.

3

The Fishermen

A siren hooted warningly. A river steamer with a single high funnel, white awnings flared over the rows of empty seats, approached the central passage between the main pylons of the bridge. Captain Tulloch, a bottle-nosed old buff, sat above the helmsman on the roof of the wheel-house, staring myopically down the narrowing channel. With its shallow draught, the steamer could glide over submerged banks barely two feet below the surface. Ransom suspected that Tulloch was now half-blind, and that his pointless passages in the empty steamer, which once carried sightseers across the lake, would go on until the craft ran immovably aground on a mud-bank.

As the steamer passed, Quilter stepped down into the water, and with an agile leap swung himself on to the hand-rail, feet in the scuppers.

'Full ahead there!' With a cry, Captain Tulloch hopped from his perch. He seized a boat-hook and hobbled down the deck towards Quilter, who grimaced at him from his hand-hold on the stern rail. Bellowing at the youth, who scuttled like a chimpanzee on its bars, Tulloch rattled the boat-hook up and down between the rails. They passed below the bridge and approached the Quilters' barge. Mrs Quilter, still fanning herself, sat up and hurled a series of vigorous epithets at the captain. Ignoring her, Tulloch drove Quilter along the rail, lunging at him like a perspiring pikeman. The helmsman swung the steamer hard by the barge, trying to rock it from its mooring. As it passed, Mrs Quilter jerked loose the line of the coracle. It bounced off the bows of the steamer, then raced like a frantic wheel between the hulls. Quilter leapt nimbly into it from the rail and was spreadeagled on the barge's deck as Captain Tulloch swung the boat-hook at his head, knocking Mrs Quilter's fan from her hand into the water.

The hot sunlight spangled in the steamer's wake as Mrs Quilter's laughter faded across it. Glad to see the old woman in such good spirits, Ransom waved to her from the deck of the houseboat, but she had followed Quilter through the hatchway. Settling itself, the river stirred slowly, now and then breaking into oily swells. Its white banks were beginning to crack like dry cement, and the shadows of the dead trees formed brittle ciphers on the slopes. Overhead a car moved along the deserted motor-bridge, heading towards the coast.

Ransom stepped out on to the jetty to inspect his rain-gauge. As he emptied the dust from the cylinder, a woman in a white beach-robe made her way down the bank fifty yards from him. She walked with the unhurried step of someone who has recovered from a long malady and feels that all the time in the world lies before her. The crumbling surface of the bank rose into the air like clouds of bone-meal. She looked down with preoccupied eyes at the thin stream of water. As she lifted her head to the sky her solitary figure seemed to Ransom like the spectre of the renascent dust.

Her strong face turned its level gaze upon Ransom, unsurprised to find him standing on the bed of the empty river. Although he had not seen her for some weeks, Ransom, conversely, knew that she would be among the last people to remain in the abandoned town. Since the death of her father, the former curator of the zoo at Mount Royal,

Catherine Austen had lived alone in the house by the river. Often Ransom saw her walking along the bank in the evening, remote sister of the lions, her long red hair reflected in the liquid colours of the water at sunset. Sometimes he called to her as he sailed past in the houseboat, but she never bothered to reply.

She knelt down by the water's edge, frowning at the dead fish and birds that drifted past. She stood up and walked across to Ransom's jetty.

She pointed to an old bucket hanging from the wooden housing of the rain-gauge. 'May I borrow that?'

Ransom handed it to her, then watched as she tried to fill it from the edge of the gangway. 'Haven't you any water left?'

'A little to drink. It's so hot, I wanted to bathe.' She lifted the bucket from the water, then decanted the dark fluid carefully into the river. The inside of the bucket was cloaked by an oily veil. Without turning, she said, 'I thought you'd gone, doctor, with everyone else, to the coast.'

Ransom shook his head. 'I've just spent a week sailing on the lake.' He pointed to the mud-flats that stretched away beyond the entrance to the river, the moisture beading on their wet slopes. 'You'll be able to walk across it soon. Are you going to stay on here?'

'Perhaps.' She watched a fishing boat enter the river and approach them, its motor beating slowly. Two men stood in the bows, scanning the deserted wharfs. A crude black awning covered the stern of the boat, where three more men sat around the tiller, their pinched faces looking across the water at Ransom, and Catherine Austen. The craft's empty nets lay amidships, but the sides of the boat had been ornamented in a way Ransom had not seen before. A large carp, slit down its belly, had been fastened to each of the rowlocks, and then turned outwards to face the water. The silver bodies of the six fish stood upright on both sides of the boat like sentinels. Ransom assumed that the boat and its crew came from one of the settlements among the marshes, and that with the drought and the end of the lake the small colonies were being drawn towards the river and Mount Royal.

Yet the significance of the mounted fish eluded him. Most of the fishermen from the marshes lived close to nature, and the carp were probably some kind of rudimentary totem, expressing the fishermen's faith in their own existence.

Catherine Austen touched his arm. 'Look at their faces.' With a smile she whispered: 'They think you're to blame.'

'For the lake?' Ransom shrugged. 'I dare say.' He watched the boat disappear below the bridge. 'Poor devils, I hope they find better catches at sea.'

'They won't leave here. Didn't you see the fish?' Catherine strolled to the end of the jetty, the white gown sweeping from her hips to the dusty boards. 'It's an interesting period – nothing moves, but so much is happening.'

'Too much. There's barely enough time to hunt for water.'

'Don't be prosaic. Water is the least of our problems.' She added: 'I take it you'll be here?'

'Why do you say that?' Ransom waited as a truck towing a large trailer crossed the bridge. 'As a matter of fact, I intend to leave in a day or two.'

Catherine gazed out at the exposed lake-bed. 'It's almost dry. Don't you feel, doctor, that everything is being drained away, all the memories and stale sentiments?'

For some reason this question, with its ironic emphasis, surprised Ransom. He looked down at the sharp eyes that watched his own. Catherine's banter seemed to conceal a complete understanding of his own thoughts. With a laugh, he raised his hands as if to fend her off. 'Do I take that as a warning? Perhaps I should change my mooring?'

'Not at all, doctor,' Catherine said blandly. 'I need you here.' She handed him the bucket. 'Have you any water to spare?'

Ransom slipped his hands into his trousers. The endless obsession with water during the previous months had forged powerful reflexes. Glad to be able to rely on them for once, he shook his head. 'I haven't. Or is that an appeal to sentiment?'

Catherine waited, and then turned away. Fastening her robe, she bent down and filled the bucket.

Ransom took her arm. He pointed to the slip road leading down from the embankment. Directly below the bridge the trailer had parked, and the families of four or five adults and half a dozen children were setting up a small camp. Two of the men carried a chemical closet out of the trailer. Followed by the children, they walked down the bank, sinking up to their knees in the white dust. When they reached the water they emptied the closet and washed it out.

'For God's sake . . . !' Catherine Austen searched the sky. 'Doctor, people are filthy.'

Ransom took the half-filled bucket from her and lowered it into the water. Catherine watched it glide away on the oily current, her face pale and expressionless. Professor Austen's wife, a noted zoologist in her own right, had died in Africa while Catherine was a child. Watching her, Ransom reflected that however isolated a man might be, women at least remained his companions, but an isolated woman was isolated absolutely.

Gathering her robe, Catherine began to make her way up the bank.

'Wait,' Ransom called. 'I'll lend you some water.' With forced humour, he added: 'You can repay me when the pressure comes on again.'

He guided her on board the houseboat and went off into

the galley. As long as the river flowed Catherine Austen remained one of its community. Besides, there were too many correspondences of character between them, more perhaps than he cared to think. However, all this would soon end. The tank in the roof contained little more than twenty-five gallons, laboriously filled from jerricans he had taken down to the river in his car. The public water supplies, a pathetic trickle all summer, had finally been discontinued three weeks earlier, and since then he had been unable to make good the constant drain on the tank.

He half-filled a can of water and carried it into the cabin. Catherine Austen was strolling up and down, inspecting his books and curios.

'You're well prepared, doctor. I see you have your own little world here. Everything outside must seem very remote.' She took the can and turned to leave. 'I'll give it back to you. I'm sure you'll need it.'

Ransom caught her elbow. The difficulties of coming to terms with the young woman warned him of all the unseen hazards of the changing landscape. 'Forget the water. Catherine, I'd hate you to think I'm smug, of all things. If I am well prepared it's just that . . .' he searched for a phrase '. . . I've always thought of the whole of life as a kind of disaster area.'

She watched him with a critical eye. 'Perhaps, but I think you've missed my point, doctor.'

She walked up the bank, and without looking back disappeared towards her villa.

Below the bridge, in the shadow of the pylons, the trailer families sat around a huge garbage fire, their faces blazing like voodoo cultists in the serpentine flames. Down on the water the solitary figure of Quilter watched them from his coracle, leaning on his pole among the dead fish like a water-borne shepherd's boy resting with his sleeping flock. As Ransom returned to the houseboat Quilter bent down and scooped a handful of the brackish water to his mouth, drank quickly and then punted himself away below the bridge with an awkward grace.

4

The Dying Swan

'Doctor! Quickly!' Half an hour later, as Ransom was fastening the galley fan-lights, there was a shout outside. A long wooden skiff, propelled by a tall, sunburnt youth, naked except for his faded cotton shorts, bumped against the houseboat, materializing like a spectre out of the canopy of reflected light that lay over the black mirror of the water.

Ransom went up on deck and found the youth, Philip Jordan, fastening the skiff fore and aft to the rail.

'What's this, Philip?' Ransom peered down into the narrow craft, where a large nest of wet mattress flock, covered with oil and cotton waste, lay in a parcel of damp newspaper.

Suddenly a snake-like head lifted from the nest and wavered at Ransom. Startled, he shouted: 'Tip it back into the water! What is it – an eel?'

'A swan, doctor!' Philip Jordan crouched down in the stern of the skiff, smoothing the clotted head and neck feathers. 'It's suffocating in the oil.' He looked up at Ransom, a hint of embarrassment in his wild eyes. 'I caught it out on the dunes and took it down to the river. I was trying to make it swim. Can you save it?'

Ransom stepped over the rail into the skiff. He searched the bird's mouth and eyes. Too exhausted to move, the swan stared up at him with its glazed orbs. The oil had matted the feathers together, and choked its mouth and respiratory passages.

Ransom stood up, shaking his head. 'Spread its wings out. I'll get some solvent from the cabin.'

'Right, doctor!'

Philip Jordan, foster-child of the river and its last presiding Ariel, lifted the bird in his arms and unfurled its wings, letting their tips fall into the water. Ransom had known him for several years, and had watched him grow from a child of twelve into a tall, long-boned youth, with the quick eyes and nervous grace of an aboriginal.

Five years earlier, when Ransom had spent his first weekends out on the lake, rebuilding his world from scratch from the materials of water, wind and sunlight, Philip Jordan had been the only person he could incorporate into his new continuum. One night, as he sat reading under a lantern in the well of his craft moored to a derelict quay among the marshes, he heard a splash of water and saw a slim brown-faced boy paddle a home-made dinghy out of the darkness. Leaving a few feet of open water between them, the boy made no reply to Ransom's questions, but watched the doctor with his wide eyes. He wore a faded khaki shirt and trousers, the remnants of an old Scout uniform. To Ransom he was part waif and part water-elf.

Ransom resumed his reading and the boy moved twenty yards away, his blade slipping in the liquid silver of the night-water. Finally he came in again and produced from between his feet a small brown owl. Raising it in his hands, he had shown it to Ransom – or more probably, the doctor guessed, had shown Ransom to the owl, the tutelary deity of his water-world – and then vanished among the reeds.

He appeared again after a lapse of one or two nights, and this time accepted the remains of a cold chicken from

Ransom. At last he replied to some of Ransom's questions, answering only those about the owl, the river and his boat. Ransom assumed he came from one of the families living in a colony of beached houseboats farther into the marshes.

He saw the boy on and off over the next year. He would share a meal with Ransom in the well of the boat, and help him sail the craft back to the entrance to the river. Here he always left Ransom, reluctant to leave the open water of the lake. Friend of the water-birds, he was able to tame swans and wild geese. He still referred to himself only by his surname, the first clue that he had escaped from some institution and he was living wild. His strange changes of costume – he would appear in a man's overcoat or pair of old shoes three sizes too big – confirmed this. During the winters he was often close to starvation, going off alone to eat the food Ransom gave him.

All these times Ransom wondered whether to report him to the police, frightened that after a cold week-end he might find the boy's body following the fish downstream. But something dissuaded him: partly his own increasing influence over Philip – he lent him paper and crayons, and helped him to read – and partly his fascination at the spectacle of this starveling of the river-ways creating his own world out of the scraps and refuse of the twentieth century, the scavenger for every nail and fish-hook turning into a wily young Ulysses of the waterfront.

As Ransom collected the turpentine and cotton waste from a locker in the galley, he reminded himself that selfishness in not reporting the youth years earlier might make Philip now pay a terrible price. The river was no more a natural environment than a handful of pebbles and water-weed in an aquarium, and its extinction would leave Philip Jordan with a repertory of skills as useless as those of a stranded fish. Philip was not a thief – but from where had come those mysterious 'gifts': clasp knives, a cigarette lighter, even an old gold-plated watch?

'Come on, doctor!' Philip Jordan beckoned him over the rail. The swan lay with wings outstretched, its plumage slick with oil.

'Easy, Philip.' Ransom began to clean the swan's bill. The bird roused faintly in response to the manual pressure, but it seemed nearly dead, smothered in the great weight of oil.

Philip Jordan shouted: 'Leave it, doctor! I'll take it down to the galley and soak off the oil.' He lifted the bird in his arms, struggling with its flopping head, but Ransom held his shoulder. 'What's the matter?'

'Philip, I can't spare the water. The bird is almost dead.'

'That's wrong, doctor!' Philip steadied himself in the skiff, the bird sliding in a sprawl out of his oil-covered arms. 'I know swans — they come back.' He released the bird and let it subside between his feet. 'Look, all I need is one bucket and some soap.'

Involuntarily, Ransom glanced up at Catherine Austen's villa. In addition to the water tank in the roof of the houseboat, there was a second tank containing two hundred gallons in the pontoon. Some inner caution had prevented him from revealing its existence to Philip Jordan.

Ransom gestured at the sky, knowing that he would have to make allowance for Philip in his plans for departure. Below his feet the dead birds and water-fowl drifted past. 'The drought may well go on for another two or three months. There's got to be an order of priorities.'

'There is, doctor!' His face stiff, Philip Jordan seized his aft line and jerked it loose. 'All right, I'll find water. The river still has plenty in it.'

'Philip, don't blame yourself.'

Ransom watched him as he paddled off, his strong arms

sweeping the skiff across the river. Standing in the stern with his legs astride, his back bending, the outstretched wings of the dying bird dipping into the water from the bows, he reminded Ransom of a land-locked mariner and his stricken albatross, deserted by the sea.

5

The Coming of the Desert

In the sunlight the white carcasses of the fish hung from their hooks in drying sheds, rotating in the warm air. The boat-houses were deserted, and the untended fishing craft were beached side by side in the shallows, their nets lying across the dust. Below the last of the wharfs two or three tons of smaller fish had been tipped out on to the bank, and the slope was covered with the silver bodies.

Turning his face from the stench, Ransom looked up at the quay. In the shadows at the back of the boat-house two of the fishermen watched him, their eyes hidden below the peaks of their caps. The other fishermen had gone, but this pair seemed content to sit there unmovingly, separated from the draining river by the dusty boat across their knees, like two widows with a coffin.

Ransom stepped through the fish, his feet sliding on their jellied skins. Fifty yards ahead he found an old dinghy on the bank that would save him the effort of crossing the motor-bridge. Pushing off, he reached the opposite shore and then retraced his steps along the bank towards Hamilton.

Across the surface of the lake the pools of evaporating water stirred in the sunlight. Along its southern margins, where the open water had given way before the drought to the creeks and marshes of Philip Jordan's water-world, the channels of damper mud wound among the white beaches. The tall columns and gantries of an experimental distillation unit operated by the municipal authorities rose above the dunes. At intervals along the shore the dark plumes of reed fires lifted into the sky from the deserted settlements, like the calligraphic signals of a primitive desert folk.

At the outskirts of the town Ransom climbed the bank and left the river, crossing an empty waterfront garden to the road behind. Unwashed by the rain, the streets were covered with dust and scraps of paper, the pavement strewn with garbage. Tarpaulins had been draped over the swimming pools, and the tattered squares lay about on the ground like ruined tents. The trim lawns shaded by willows and plane trees, the avenues of miniature palms and rhododendrons had vanished, leaving a clutter of ramshackle gardens. Most of Ransom's neighbours had joined the exodus to the coast. Already Hamilton was a desert town, built on an isthmus of sand between a drained lake and a forgotten river, sustained by a few meagre waterholes.

Two or three months beforehand many of the residents had built wooden towers in their gardens, some of them thirty or forty feet high, equipped with small observation platforms to give them an uninterrupted view of the southern horizon. From this quadrant alone were any clouds expected to appear, generated from moisture evaporated off the surface of the sea.

Halfway down Columbia Drive, as he looked up at the deserted towers, a passing car swerved in front of Ransom, forcing him on to the pavement. It stopped twenty yards ahead.

'Ransom, is that you? Do you want a lift?'

Ransom crossed the road, recognizing the grey-haired man in a clerical collar – the Reverend Howard Johnstone, minister of the Presbyterian Church at Hamilton.

Johnstone opened the door and moved a shot-gun along the seat, peering at Ransom with a sharp eye.

'I nearly ran you down,' he told Ransom, beckoning him to shut the door before he had seated himself. 'Why the devil are you wearing that beard? There's nothing to hide from.'

'Of course not, Howard,' Ransom agreed. 'It's purely penitential. Actually, I thought it suited me.'

'It doesn't. Let me assure you of that.'

A man of vigorous and stubborn temper, the Reverend Johnstone was one of those muscular clerics who intimidate their congregations not so much by the prospect of divine justice at some future date but by the threat of immediate physical retribution in the here and now. Well over six feet tall, his strong head topped by a fierce crown of grey hair, he towered over his parishioners from his pulpit, eyeing each of them in their pews like a bad-tempered headmaster obliged to take a junior form for one day and determined to inflict the maximum of benefit upon them. His long twisted jaw gave all his actions an air of unpredictability, but during the previous months he had become almost the last pillar of the lakeside community. Ransom found his bellicose manner hard to take – something about the suspicious eyes and lack of charity made him doubtful of the minister's motives – but none the less he was glad to see him. At Johnstone's initiative a number of artesian wells had been drilled and a local militia recruited, ostensibly to guard the church and property of his parishioners, but in fact to keep out the transients moving along the highway to the south.

Recently a curious streak had emerged in Johnstone's character. He had developed a fierce moral contempt for those who had given up the fight against the drought and retreated to the coast. In a series of fighting sermons preached during the last three or four Sundays he had warned his listeners of the offence they would be committing by opting out of the struggle against the elements. By a strange logic he seemed to believe that the battle against the drought, like that against evil itself, was the local responsibility of every community and private individual throughout the land, and that a strong element of rivalry was to be encouraged between the contestants, brother set against brother, in order to keep the battle joined.

Notwithstanding all this, most of his flock had deserted him, but Johnstone stayed on in his embattled church, preaching his sermons to a congregation of barely half a dozen people.

'Have you been in hiding for the last week?' he asked Ransom. 'I thought you'd gone.'

'Not at all, Howard,' Ransom assured him. 'I went off on a fishing trip. I had to get back for your sermon this Sunday.'

'Don't mock me, Charles. Not yet. A last-minute repentance may be better than nothing, but I expect rather more from you.' He held Ransom's arm in a powerful grip. 'It's good to see you. We need everyone we can muster.'

Ransom looked out at the deserted avenue. Most of the houses were empty, windows boarded and nailed up, swimming pools emptied of their last reserves of water. Lines of abandoned cars were parked under the withering plane trees and the road was littered with discarded cans and cartons. The bright flint-like dust lay in drifts against the fences. Refuse fires smouldered unattended on the burnt-out lawns, their smoke wandering over the roofs.

'I'm glad I stayed out of the way,' Ransom said. 'Has everything been quiet?'

'Yes and no. We've had a few spots of trouble. I'm on my way to something now, as a matter of fact.'

'What about the police rearguard? Has it gone yet?'

Despite the careful offhandedness of Ransom's question,

Johnstone smiled knowingly. 'It leaves today, Charles. You'll have time to say goodbye to Judith. However, you ought to make her stay.'

'I couldn't if I wanted to.' Ransom sat forward and pointed through the windscreen. 'What's this?'

They turned into Amherst Avenue and stopped by the church at the corner. A group of five or six men, members of Johnstone's parish militia, stood around a dusty green saloon car, shouting at the driver. Tempers flared in the brittle light, and the men rocked the car from side to side, drumming on the roof with their rifles. Fists began to fly, and a sturdy square-shouldered man wearing a dirty panama hat hurled himself at the men like a berserk terrier. As he disappeared from sight in the mêlée a woman's voice cried out.

Seizing his shot-gun, Johnstone set off towards them, Ransom behind him. The owner of the saloon was struggling with three men who held him down on his knees. As someone shouted 'Here's the Reverend!' he looked up from the ground with fierce determination, like a heretic forced to unwilling prayer. Watching helplessly from the front seat of the car was a small moon-faced woman. Behind her, the white faces of three children, one a boy of eight, peered through the side window among the bundles and suitcases.

Johnstone pulled the men apart, the shot-gun raised in the air. His burly figure was a good head taller than the others.

'That's enough! I'll deal with him now!' He lifted the driver to his feet with one hand. 'Who is he? What's he been up to?'

Edward Gunn, owner of the local hardware store, stepped forward, an accusing finger raised in front of his beaked grey face. 'I caught him in the church, Reverend, with a bucket. He was taking water from the font.'

'The font?' Johnstone gazed down magisterially at the little driver. With heavy sarcasm he bellowed: 'Did you want to be baptized? Is that what you wanted, before all the water in the world was gone?'

The stocky man pushed Gunn aside. 'No, I wanted water to drink! We've come three hundred miles today – look at my kids, they're so dry they can't even weep!' He opened his leather wallet and spread out a fan of greasy bills. 'I'm not asking for charity, I'll pay good money.'

Johnstone brushed aside the money with the barrel of the shot-gun. 'We take no cash for water here, son. You can't buy off the droughts of this world, you have to fight them. You should have stayed where you were, in your own home.'

'That's right!' Edward Gunn cut in. 'Get back to your own neighbourhood!'

The stocky man spat in disgust. 'My own neighbourhood is six hundred miles away, it's nothing but dust and dead cattle!'

Ransom stepped over to him. Johnstone's bullying presence seemed merely to aggravate their difficulties. To the owner of the saloon he said: 'Quieten down. I'll give you some water.' He tore a sheet from an old prescription pad in his pocket and pointed to the address. 'Drive around the block and park by the river, then walk down to my house. All right?'

'Well . . .' The man eyed Ransom suspiciously, then relaxed. 'Thanks a lot, I'm glad to see there's one here, at least.' He picked his panama hat off the groud, straightened the brim and dusted it off. Nodding pugnaciously to Johnstone, he climbed into the car and drove away.

Gunn and his fellow vigilantes dispersed among the dead trees, sauntering down the lines of cars.

As he settled his large frame behind the wheel Johnstone said: 'Kind of you, Charles, but begging the question. There are few places in this country where there aren't small supplies of local water, if you work hard enough for them.'

'I know,' Ransom said. 'But see it from his point of view. Thousands of cattle dead in the fields – to these poor farming people it must seem like the end of the world.'

Johnstone drummed a fist on the wheel. 'That's not for us to decide! There are too many people now living out their own failures, that's the secret appeal of this drought. I was going to give the fellow some water, Charles, but I wanted him to show more courage first.'

'Of course,' Ransom said noncommittally. Five minutes earlier he had been glad to see Johnstone, but he realized that the clergyman was imposing his own fantasies on the changing landscape, as he himself had done. He was relieved when Johnstone let him out at the end of the avenue.

On the right, overlooking the mouth of the river as it entered the lake, was the glass-and-concrete mansion owned by Richard Foster Lomax. At one end of the outdoor swimming pool a fountain threw rainbows of light through the air. Taking his ease at the edge of the pool was the strutting figure of Lomax, hands in the pockets of his white silk suit, his ironic voice calling to someone in the water.

Johnstone pointed at Lomax. 'Much as I detest Lomax, he does prove my point.' As a parting shot, he leaned out of the window and called after Ransom: 'Remember, Charles, charity shouldn't be too easy to give!'

6

The Crying Land

Musing on this callous but shrewd criticism of his own motives, Ransom walked home along the deserted avenue. In the drive outside the house his car stood by the garage door, but for some reason he found it difficult to recognize, as if he were returning home after a lapse not merely of a week but of several years. A light coating of dust covered the bodywork and seats, as if the car were already a distant memory of itself, the lapsed time condensing on it like dew. This softening of outlines could be seen in the garden, the fine silt on the swing-seats and metal table blurring their familiar profiles. The sills and gutters of the house were covered with the same ash, blunting the image of it in his mind. Watching the dust accumulate against the walls, Ransom could almost see it several years ahead, reverting to a primitive tumulus, a mastaba of white ash in which a forgotten nomad had once made his home.

He let himself into the house, noticing the small shoe-marks that carried the dust across the carpet, fading as they reached the stairs like the footprint of someone returning from the future. For a moment, as he looked at the furniture in the hall, Ransom was tempted to open the windows and let the wind inundate everything, obliterating the past, but fortunately, during the previous years, both he and Judith had used the house as little more than a pied à terre.

On the hall floor below the letter-box he found a thick envelope of government circulars. Ransom carried them into the lounge. He sat down in an armchair and looked out through the french windows at the bleached dust-bowl that had once been his lawn. Beyond the withered hedges his neighbour's watch-tower rose into the air, but the smoke from the refuse fires veiled the view of the lake and river.

He glanced at the circulars. These described, successively, the end of the drought and the success of the rain-seeding operations, the dangers of drinking sea-water, and, lastly, the correct procedure for reaching the coast.

He stood up and wandered around the house, uncertain how to begin the task of mobilizing its resources. In the refrigerator melted butter dripped on to the tray below. The smells of sour milk and bad meat made him close the door. A stock of canned foods and cereals stood on the pantry shelves, and a small reserve of water lay in the roof tank, but this was due less to foresight than to the fact that, like himself, Judith took most of her meals out.

The house reflected this domestic and personal vacuum. The neutral furniture and decorations were as anonymous and free of associations as those of a motel – indeed, Ransom realized, they had been unconsciously selected for just this reason. In a sense the house was a perfect model of a spatio-temporal vacuum, inserted into the continuum of his life by the private alternate universe in the houseboat on the river. Walking about the house he felt more like a forgotten visitor than its owner, a shadowy and ever more evasive double of himself.

The radiogram sat inertly beside the empty fireplace. Ransom switched it on and off, and then remembered an old transistor radio which Judith had bought. He went upstairs to her bedroom. Most of her cosmetic bric-à-brac had been cleared away from the dressing table, and a single line of empty bottles was reflected in the mirror. In the centre of the bed lay a large blue suitcase, crammed to the brim.

Ransom stared down at it. Although its significance was obvious, he found himself, paradoxically, wondering whether Judith was at last coming to stay with him. Ironic inversions of this type, rather than scenes of bickering frustration, had characterized the slow winding-down of their marriage, like the gradual exhaustion of an enormous clock that at times, relativistically, appeared to be running backwards.

There was a tentative tap on the kitchen door. Ransom went downstairs and found the owner of the green saloon, hat in his hands. With a nod, he stepped into the kitchen. He walked about stiffly, as if unused to being inside a house. 'Are your family all right?' Ransom asked.

'Just about. Who's that crackpot down by the lake?'

'The concrete house with the swimming pool? – one of the local eccentrics. I shouldn't worry about him.'

'He's the one who should be worrying,' the little man retorted. 'Anyone that crazy is going to be in trouble soon.'

He waited as Ransom filled a two-gallon can from the sink tap. There was no pressure and the water dribbled in. When Ransom handed him the can he seemed to switch himself on, as if he had suspended judgment on the possibility of receiving the water until it made physical contact with his hands.

'It's good of you, doctor. Grady's the name, Matthew Grady. This'll keep the kids going to the coast.'

'Drink some yourself. You look as if you need it. It's only a hundred miles.'

Grady nodded sceptically. 'Maybe. But I figure the last couple of miles will be really hard going. Could take us a whole two days, maybe three. You can't drink sea-water. Getting down on to the beach is only the start.' At the door he added, as if the water in his hand compelled him to reciprocate at least a modicum of good advice: 'Doctor, things are going to be rough soon. You pull out now while you can.'

Ransom smiled at this. 'I already have pulled out. Anyway, keep a place for me on the sand.' He watched Grady wrap the can in his coat and bob off down the drive, eyes moving from left to right as he slipped away between the cars.

Unable to relax in the empty house, Ransom decided to wait for Judith in the drive. The fine ash settled through the air from the unattended fires, and he climbed into the car, dusting the seats and controls. He switched on the radio and listened to the intermittent news reports broadcast from the few radio stations still operating.

The world-wide drought now in its fifth month was the culmination of a series of extended droughts that had taken place with increasing frequency all over the globe during the previous decade. Ten years earlier a critical shortage of world food-stuffs had occurred when the seasonal rainfall expected in a number of important agricultural areas had failed to materialize. One by one, areas as far apart as Saskatchewan and the Loire valley, Kazakhstan and the Madras tea country were turned into arid dust-basins. The following months brought little more than a few inches of rain, and after two years these farmlands were totally devastated. Once their populations had resettled themselves elsewhere, these new deserts were abandoned for good.

The continued appearance of more and more such areas on the map, and the added difficulties of making good the world's food supplies, led to the first attempts at some form of global weather control. A survey by the UN Food and Agriculture Organization showed that everywhere river levels and water tables were falling. The two-and-a-half million square miles drained by the Amazon had shrunk to less than half this area. Scores of its tributaries had dried up completely, and aerial surveys discovered that much of the former rainforest was already dry and petrified. At Khartoum, in lower Egypt, the White Nile was twenty feet below its mean level ten years earlier, and lower outlets were bored in the concrete barrage of the dam at Aswan.

Despite world-wide attempts at cloud-seeding, the amounts of rainfall continued to diminish. The seeding operations finally ended when it was obvious that not only was there no rain, but there were no clouds. At this point attention switched to the ultimate source of rainfall – the ocean surface. It needed only the briefest scientific examination to show that here were the origins of the drought.

Covering the off-shore waters of the world's oceans, to a distance of about a thousand miles from the coast, was a thin but resilient mono-molecular film formed from a complex of saturated long-chain polymers, generated within the sea from the vast quantities of industrial wastes discharged into the ocean basins during the previous fifty years. This tough, oxygen-permeable membrane lay on the air–water interface and prevented almost all evaporation of surface water into the air space above. Although the structure of these polymers was quickly identified, no means was found of removing them. The saturated linkages produced in the perfect organic bath of the sea were completely non-reactive, and formed an intact seal broken only when the water was violently disturbed. Fleets of trawlers and naval craft equipped with rotating flails began to ply up and down the Atlantic and Pacific coasts of North America, and along the sea-boards of Western Europe, but without any long-term effects. Likewise, the removal of the entire surface water provided only a temporary respite – the film quickly replaced itself by lateral extension from the surrounding surface, recharged by precipitation from the reservoir below.

The mechanism of formation of these polymers remained obscure, but millions of tons of highly reactive industrial wastes – unwanted petroleum fractions, contaminated catalysts and solvents – were still being vented into the sea, where they mingled with the wastes of atomic power stations and sewage schemes. Out of this brew the sea had constructed a skin no thicker than a few atoms, but sufficiently strong to devastate the lands it once irrigated.

This act of retribution by the sea had always impressed Ransom by its simple justice. Cetyl alcohol films had long been used as a means of preventing evaporation from water reservoirs, and nature had merely extended the principle, applying a fractional tilt, at first imperceptible, to the balance of the elements. As if further to tantalize mankind, the billowing cumulus clouds, burdened like madonnas with cool rain, which still formed over the central ocean surfaces, would sail steadily towards the shorelines but always deposit their cargo into the dry unsaturated air above the sealed offshore waters, never on to the crying land.

7

The Face

A police car approached along the avenue and stopped fifty yards away. After a discreet interval, stemming more from custom than any sense of propriety, Judith Ransom stepped out. She leaned through the window, talking to Captain Hendry. After checking her watch against his, she hurried up the drive. She failed to notice Ransom sitting in the dust-covered car, and went on into the house.

Ransom waited until she had gone upstairs. He stepped from the car and strolled down towards Hendry. Ransom had always liked the police captain, and during the past two years their relationship had become the most stable side of the triangle — indeed, Ransom sometimes guessed, its main bond. How long Judith and Hendry would survive the rigours of the beach alone remained to be seen.

As Ransom reached the car Hendry put down the map he was studying.

'Still here, Charles? Don't you feel like a few days at the beach?'

'I can't swim.' Ransom pointed to the camping equipment in the back seat. 'All that looks impressive. A side of Judith's character I never managed to explore.'

'I haven't either — yet. Perhaps it's just wishful thinking. Do I have your blessing?'

'Of course. And Judith too, you know that.'

Hendry gazed up at Ransom. 'You sound completely

detached, Charles. What are you planning to do – wait here until the place turns into a desert?'

Ransom drew his initials in the dust behind the windscreen wiper. 'It seems to be a desert already. Perhaps I'm more at home here. I want to stay on a few days and find out.'

'Rather you than me. Do you think you really will leave?'

'Certainly. It's just a whim of mine, you know.'

But something about Hendry's changed tone, the note of condescension, reminded Ransom that Hendry might resent his sense of detachment more than he imagined. He talked to the captain for a few minutes, then said goodbye and went indoors.

He found Judith in the kitchen, rooting in the refrigerator. A small stack of cans stood in a carton on the table.

'Charles—' She straightened up, brushing her blonde hair off her angular face. 'That beard – I thought you were down at the river.'

'I was,' Ransom said. 'I came back to see if I could do anything for us. It's rather late in the day.'

Judith watched him with a neutral expression. 'Yes, it is,' she said matter-of-factly. She bent down to the refrigerator again, flicking at the greasy cans with her well-tended nails.

'I've been dividing things up,' she explained. 'I've left you most of the stuff. And you can have all the water.'

Ransom watched her seal the carton, then search for string in the cupboard, sweeping the tail of her linen coat off the floor. Her departure, like his own from the house, involved no personal component whatsoever. Their relationship was now completely functional, like that of two technicians who had successfully tried to install a complex domestic appliance.

'I'll get your suitcase.' She said nothing, but her grey eyes followed him to the stairs.

When he came down she was waiting in the hall. She

picked up the carton. 'Charles, what are you going to do?'

Despite himself, Ransom laughed. In a sense the question had been prompted by his beachcomber-like appearance and beard, but the frequency with which he had been asked it by so many different people made him realize that his continued presence in the deserted town, his apparent acceptance of the silence and emptiness, in some way exposed the vacuum in their lives.

He wondered whether to try to convey to Judith his involvement with the changing role of the landscape and river, their metamorphosis in time and memory. Catherine Austen would have understood his preoccupations, and accepted that for Ransom the only final rest from the persistence of memory would come from his absolution in time. But Judith, as he knew, hated all mention of the subject, and for good reason. Woman's role in time was always tenuous and uncertain.

Her pale face regarded his shadow on the wall, as if searching for some last clue in this map-like image. Then he saw that she was watching herself in the mirror. He noticed again the marked lack of symmetry in her face, the dented left temple that she tried to disguise with a fold of hair. It was as if her face already carried the injuries of an appalling motor-car accident that would happen somewhere in the future. Sometimes Ransom felt that Judith was aware of this herself, and moved through life with this grim promise always before her.

She opened the door on to the dusty drive. 'Good luck, Charles. Look after that Jordan boy.'

'He'll be looking after me.'

'I know. You need him, Charles.'

As they went out into the drive enormous black clouds were crossing the sky from the direction of Mount Royal.

'Good God!' Judith started to run down the drive, dropping her bag. 'Is that rain?'

Ransom caught up with her. He peered at the billows of smoke rising from the dark skyline of the city. 'Don't worry. It's the city. It's on fire.'

After she and Hendry had gone he went back to the house, the image of Judith's face still in his eyes. She had looked back at him with an expression of horror, as if frightened that she was about to lose everything she had gained.

8

The Fire Sermon

For the next three days the fires continued to burn in
Mount Royal. Under a sky stained by an immense pall of
black smoke, like a curtain drawn over the concluding act
of the city, the long plumes rose high into the air, drifting
away like the fragments of an enormous collapsing message.
Mingled with the fires of incinerators and abandoned garbage, they transformed the open plain beyond the city into
an apocalyptic landscape.

From the roof of his house, Ransom watched the motor-
bridge across the river, waiting for the last inhabitants of
the city to leave for the south. By now Hamilton was empty.
With the exception of the Reverend Johnstone and his last
parishioners, all Ransom's neighbours had gone. He strolled
among the deserted streets, watching the dust columns
rising into the sky from a landscape that seemed to be on
fire. The light, ashy dust blown across the lakeside town
from the hundreds of incinerators on the outskirts of the
city covered the streets and gardens like the fall-out from
a volcano.

Much of the time Ransom spent by the river, or walking
out across the bed of the lake. Inshore, the slopes of damp
mud had already dried into a series of low dunes, their
crests yellowing in the heat. Wandering among them, out
of sight of the town, Ransom found the hulks of sunken
yachts and barges, their blurred forms raised from the

weary limbo to await the judgment of the sun. Ransom built a crude raft out of pieces of driftwood and punted himself across the lagoons of brackish water, making his way in a wide circle back towards the river.

Although still narrowing, the channel was too deep to ford. As viscous and oily as black treacle, it leaked slowly between the white banks. Only the elusive figure of Philip Jordan, punting his arrow-like skiff in and out of the thermal pools, gave it any movement. Once or twice Ransom called to him, but the youth waved and vanished with a glimmer of his pole, intent on some private errand. A few craft sat on the surface, reflected in the sinking mirror. At intervals throughout the day a siren would give a mournful hoot, and the old steamer, still commanded by Captain Tulloch, would make its way up-river. Then, with another hoot, it would move off into the haze over the lake, disappearing among the narrow creeks.

It was during this time that Ransom again became aware of the significance of each day. Perhaps this was because he knew he would be able to stay on in Hamilton for a further two or three weeks at the most. After that, whatever happened, and even if he chose to stay behind, his existence would be determined by a new set of rules, probably those of chase and pursuit. But until then a finite period remained, the unending sequence of day following day had given way to a sharply defined quantum of existence. Superficially the streets and houses resembled those of the normal world. The lines that once marked its boundaries still formed a discreet but unreal image, like the false object seen in a convex mirror.

To his surprise, however, Ransom felt little urge to visit his houseboat. It remained quietly at its mooring, the condensation of a distant private universe.

On Sunday, the last day of this short interregnum, Ransom visited the Presbyterian church on the corner of

Amherst Avenue to hear what he assumed to be the Reverend Johnstone's concluding sermon. During this period the minister had been busy with the few remaining members of his militia, driving about in his jeep with bales of barbed wire and crates of supplies, fortifying their houses for use as strongpoints in the final Armageddon to come. Curious to see how Johnstone was responding to the transformation of Hamilton and the city, Ransom walked down to the church and entered the aisle just as the small, manually operated organ concluded its short voluntary.

He took his seat in one of the pews halfway down the nave. Johnstone left the organ and began to read the lesson from the lectern. The church was almost empty, and Johnstone's strong voice, as belligerent as ever, reverberated off the empty pews. Below him, in the front row, sat his small, dove-haired wife and three unmarried daughters, wearing their floral hats. Behind them were the two or three families who still remained, the men's shot-guns discreetly out of view.

After the hymn, Johnstone mounted the pulpit and began his sermon, taking as his text Chapter IV, Verse 8, of the Book of Jonah: 'And it came to pass, when the sun did arise, that God prepared a vehement east wind; and the sun beat upon the head of Jonah, that he fainted, and wished in himself to die, and said, It is better for me to die than to live.' After a brief résumé of the previous career of Jonah, whose desire for the early destruction of Nineveh and the Gentiles he seemed generally to approve, Johnstone went on to compare the booth the Lord had built for Jonah to the east of Nineveh with the church in whose safety they now sat, waiting for the destruction of Mount Royal and the world beyond.

At this point, as Johnstone warmed to his theme, he glanced down the nave with a slight start. Ransom looked over his shoulder. Standing between the pews at the rear of the church, caps in hand, were some twenty of the fishermen, their thin faces staring down the aisle at the pulpit. For a few moments they stood together, listening to Johnstone as he drew breath and continued his peroration. Then they shuffled into the pews at the back. Exposed behind them through the open door, the billows of smoke drifted across the roof-tops from Mount Royal.

Surprised by their visit to the church, in their black shabby clothes and old boots, Ransom moved down to the end of the pew, from where he could glance back at the fishermen. Their faces had the closed expressions of a group of strikers or unemployed, biding their time until given the word to act.

Below the pulpit there were whispered exchanges, and a gun barrel moved uneasily, but the Reverend Johnstone took the new arrivals in his stride. His eyes roved along the lines of sullen faces. Raising his voice, he recapitulated what he had said so far. Then he went on to expand upon his theme, comparing Jonah's wish for the destruction of Nineveh with mankind's unconscious hopes for the end of their present world. Just as the withering of Jonah's gourd by the worm was part of the Lord's design, so they themselves should welcome the destruction of their homes and livelihoods, and even their very shelter from the drought, knowing that God's grace would come to them only through this final purging fire.

The fishermen's eyes were fixed on Johnstone's face. One or two leaned forward, hands clasping the pew in front, but most of them sat upright. Johnstone paused before his homily, and there was a brief shuffle. The entire group of fishermen rose to their feet, and without a backward glance made their way from the church.

The Reverend Johnstone stopped to let them go, quietening the front pews with a raised hand. He eyed the retreating figures with his head to one side, as if trying to sum up their motives for coming to the church. Then, in a lower voice, he called his depleted congregation to prayer, glancing through his raised hands at the open doors.

Ransom waited, and then slipped away down the aisle and stepped out into the sunlight. In the distance he caught a last glimpse of the black-clad figures moving between the cars, the smoke clouds crossing the avenue over their heads.

At his feet, traced in the white dust on the pavement outside the porch, was a small fish-shaped sign.

9

The Phoenix

'Doctor.'

As Ransom knelt down to examine the sign a hand like a bird's claw clasped his shoulder. He looked up to find the broad, dented face of Quilter gazing at him with moist eyes.

'Lomax,' he said by way of introduction. 'He wants you. Now.'

Ransom ignored him and followed the loop in the dust with his finger. Quilter leaned against the stump of a tree, listening with a bored expression to the faint sounds of the organ from the church. His ragged clothes were stained with tar and wine.

Ransom stood up, brushing his hands. 'What's the matter with Lomax?'

Quilter looked him up and down. '*You* tell him,' he said offensively. When Ransom refused to be provoked his broken face relaxed into a smile, first of grudging respect, which became more and more twisted until all humour had gone and only a bitter parody remained. He tapped his head slyly and said, *sotto voce*: 'Perhaps . . . water on the brain?' With a laugh he made off down the avenue, beckoning Ransom after him and pointing with his forefinger at the observation platforms on the watch-towers.

Ransom followed him at an interval, on the way collecting his valise from his house. Quilter's oblique comment on Lomax, probably a tip of some sort, might well contain more truth than most people would have given him credit for. Lomax was certainly an obsessed character, and the drought and its infinite possibilities had no doubt inflamed his imagination beyond all limits.

At the gates Quilter pulled a bunch of keys from his pocket. He unleashed the two Alsatians fastened to the iron grille. Giving each of them a hard kick in the rump to quieten it down, he led the way up the drive. Lomax's house, a glass-and-concrete folly, stood above them on its circular embankment, the balconies and aerial verandas reflecting the sunlight like the casements of a jewelled glacier. The lines of sprinklers had been switched off and the turf was streaked with yellow, the burnt ochre of the soil showing through at the edge of the coloured tile pathways. Alongside the swimming pool a large green tanker was pumping the remains of the water out through a convoluted metal hose. The diesel thumped with a low monotonous thirst. From the cabin the driver watched with weary eyes as the ornamental floor appeared.

The hallway, however, was pleasantly cool. A set of wet footprints crossed the marble squares.

Lomax was in his suite on the first floor. He sat back against the bolster on the gilt bed, fully dressed in his white silk suit, like a pasha waiting for his court to assemble. Without moving his head, he waved his silver-topped cane at Ransom.

'Do come in, Charles,' he called in his clipped, creamy voice. 'How kind of you, I feel better already.' He tapped the wicker rocking chair beside the bed. 'Sit down here where I can see you.' Still not moving his head, he shook his cane at Quilter, who stood grinning in the doorway. 'All right, my boy, away with you! There's work to be done. If you find those lackeys of mine, turn the dogs on them!'

When Quilter had gone, the Alsatians pawing frantically at the floor in the hall, Lomax inclined his head at Ransom. His small face wore an expression of puckish charm.

'My dear Charles, I do apologize for sending Quilter to you, but the servants have left me. Can you believe it, the ingratitude! But the Gadarene rush is on, nothing will stop them . . .' He sighed theatrically, then winked at Ransom and confided coarsely: 'Bloody fools, aren't they? What are they going to do when they get to the sea – swim?'

He sat back with a rictus of affected pain and gazed limply at the decorated ceiling, like a petulant Nero overwhelmed by the absurdity and ingratitude of the world. Ransom watched the performance with a tolerant smile. The pose, he knew, was misleading. Under the cupid-like exterior Lomax's face was hard and rapacious.

'What's the matter?' Ransom asked him. 'You look all right.'

'Well, I'm not, Charles.' Lomax raised his cane and gestured towards his right ear. 'A drop of water from that confounded pool jumped into it; for a day I've been carrying the Atlantic Ocean around in my head. I feel as if I'm turning into an oyster.'

He waited, eyes half-closed with pleasure, as Ransom sat back and laughed at the intended irony of this. Ransom was one of the few people to appreciate his Fabergé style without any kind of moral reservation – everyone else was faintly shocked, for which Lomax despised them ('mankind's besetting sin, Charles,' he once complained, 'is to sit in judgment on its fellows'), or viewed him uneasily from a distance. In part this reaction was based on an instinctive revulsion from Lomax's ambiguous physical make-up, and the sense that his whole personality was based on, and even exploited, precisely these areas.

Yet Ransom felt that this was to misjudge him. Just as his own stratified personality reflected his preoccupation with the vacuums and drained years of his memory, so Lomax's had been formed by his intense focus upon the immediate present, his crystallization on the razor's edge of the momentary impulse. In a sense, he was a super-saturation of himself, the elegant cartouches of his nostrils and the waves of his pomaded hair like the decoration on a baroque pavilion, containing a greater ambient time than defined by its own space. Suitably pricked, he would probably begin to deliquesce, fizzing out in a brilliant sparkle of contained light.

Ransom opened his valise. 'All right, let's have a look. Perhaps I'll find a pearl.'

When Lomax settled himself, he examined the ear and syringed it, then pronounced it sound.

'I'm so relieved, Charles, it's your neutral touch. Hippocrates would have been proud of you.' Lomax eyed Ransom for a moment, and then continued, his voice more pointed: 'While you're here there's another little matter I wanted to raise with you. I've been so busy recently with one thing and another, I haven't had a chance until now.' Steadying himself with the cane, he lowered his short legs to the floor, accepting Ransom's hand with a flourish of thanks.

Despite Lomax's pose as an elderly invalid, Ransom could feel the hard muscles beneath the smooth silk suiting, and noted the supple ease with which he moved off across the floor. What exactly had kept him busy Ransom could only guess. The dapper white shoes and spotless suit indicated a fairly insulated existence during the previous weeks. Perhaps Lomax saw an opportunity to settle some old scores. Although responsible for a concert hall and part of the university in Mount Royal – examples of his Japanese, pagoda-ridden phase some years earlier – Lomax had long been persona non grata with the local authorities. No doubt he had been brooding over his revenge for the way they had allowed a firm of commercial builders to complete the university project after local conservative opinion, outraged by the glass minarets and tiled domes rising over their heads, had marched on the city hall. But the officials concerned would by now be safely at the coast, well out of Lomax's reach.

'What's on your mind?' Ransom asked, as Lomax sprayed the air with a few puffs of scent from a gilt plunger on his dressing table.

'Well, Charles . . .' Lomax gazed out at the obscured skyline of the city, from which the smoke rose more and more thickly. To his right the bleached white bed of the river wound its way between the riverside villas. 'What's going on out there? You know more about these things than I do.'

Ransom gestured at the windows. 'It's plain enough. You really must have been busy if you haven't noticed. The entire balance of nature has—'

Lomax snapped his fingers irritably. 'Don't talk to me about the balance of nature! If it wasn't for people like myself we'd all be living in mud huts.' He peered darkly at the city. 'A good thing too, judging by that – I mean what's happening over there, in Mount Royal? I take it most people have left?'

'Nine out of ten of them. Probably more. There can't be much future for them there.'

'That's where you're wrong. There's a great deal of future there, believe me.' He walked towards Ransom, his head on one side, like a couturier inspecting a suspect mannequin, about to remove a single pin and expose the whole shabby pretence. 'And what about you, Charles? I can't understand why you haven't set off for the coast with everyone else?'

'Can't you, Richard? I think you probably can. Perhaps we both have some unfinished business to clear up.'

Lomax nodded sagely. 'Well put, with your usual tact. I hate to pry, but I care for you in a strange sort of way. You began with so many advantages in life — advantages of character, I mean — and you've deliberately ignored them. There's a true nobility, the Roman virtue. Unlike myself, I haven't a moral notion in my head.' Thoughtfully, he added: 'Until now, that is. I feel I may at last be coming into my own. Still, what are you actually going to do? You can't just sit on the mud in your little houseboat.'

'I haven't been there for three or four days,' Ransom said. 'The roads are crowded, I felt I could better come to terms with certain problems here. I'll have to leave eventually.'

'Perhaps. Certainly everything is going to be very changed here, Charles.'

Ransom lifted his valise off the floor. 'I've grasped that much.' He pointed to the dusty villas along the river. 'They look like mud huts already. We're moving straight back into the past.'

Lomax shook his head. 'You've got your sense of direction wrong, my boy. It's the future each of us has to come to terms with now.' He straightened up. 'Why don't you come and live here?'

'Thank you, Richard, no.'

'Why not?' Lomax pressed. 'Let's be honest, you don't intend to leave — I can see that in your face a mile off. The servants will be back soon, for one damn good reason, if no other—' his eyes flashed knowingly at Ransom '—they're going to find the sea isn't quite so full of water as they think. Back to old Father Neptune, yes. They'll look after you, and Quilter's a willing lad, full of strange notions, though a bit tiresome at times. You'll be able to moon around, come to terms with Judith—'

Ransom walked to the door. 'Richard, I have already. A long time ago. It's you who's missing the point now.'

'Wait!' Lomax scurried after him. 'Those of us staying behind have got to rally together, Charles. I'm damned if I'm going to the sea. All that water, a mineral I despise, utterly unmalleable, fit only for fountains. Also, you'll be able to help me with a little project of mine.'

'What's that?'

'Well . . .' Lomax glanced slyly in the direction of the city. 'A slight divertissement I've been toying with. Rather spectacular, as a matter of fact. I'd tell you, Charles, but it's probably best to wait until we're more committed to each other.'

'Very wise of you.' Ransom watched Lomax pivoting on his white shoes, obviously delighted with the idea and only just managing to keep it to himself. The billows of red smoke rose from the city, reflected in Lomax's suit and puckish face, and for a moment transforming him into a plump, grinning Mephistopheles.

'What are you planning to do?' Ransom asked. 'Burn the city down?'

'Charles . . .' A smile crossed Lomax's face like a slow crack around a vase. 'That's a suggestion worth bearing in mind. What a pity Quilter isn't here, he adores ideas like that.'

'I dare say.' Ransom went over to the door.

This time Lomax made no attempt to stop him. 'You know, your idea touches my imagination! Great fires have always been the prelude to even greater futures.' He gazed out at the city. 'What a phoenix!'

10

Miranda

Ransom left him rhapsodizing on this notion. As he crossed the hall the last sounds of the tanker's pump came from the swimming pool.

'Quilty! Is that you, Quilty?' A woman's voice called sleepily from the veranda overlooking the swimming pool.

Ransom stopped, recognizing the sharp, child-like tone. Trying to disguise his footsteps, he walked on towards the door.

'Quilty! What are you creeping around for – oh! Who the hell are you?'

Miranda Lomax, the architect's sister, her white hair falling like a shawl around her robe, stood barefoot in the entrance to the hall, scrutinizing Ransom with her small eyes. Although twenty years younger than Lomax – but was she really his sister, Ransom sometimes speculated, or a distant cousin, the cast-off partner in an ambiguous *ménage à deux* – her face was a perfect replica of Lomax's, with its puckish cheeks, hard eyes and the mouth of a corrupt Cupid. Her long hair, white as the ash now settling on the lawn outside, made her look prematurely aged, and she was in fact like a wise, evil child. On their occasional meetings, when she arrived, chauffeur-driven, at the hospital on some unspecified errand, Ransom always felt a sharp sense of unease, although superficially she was attractive enough. Perhaps this physical appeal, the gilding of the diseased lily, was what warned him away from her. Lomax's eccentricities were predictable in their way, but Miranda was less self-immersed, casting her eye on the world like a witch waiting for the casual chance.

'Dr Ransom . . .' Visibly let down, she turned to go back to the veranda. Then, out of boredom, she beckoned him across the hall. 'You look tired, doctor.' She slouched off, the soiled beach-wrap trailing behind her.

The double windows were sealed to keep out the dust, and obscured the green hull of the tanker at the far end of the pool. Despite its length the veranda was claustrophobic, the air dead and unoccupied. A peculiar scent hung about, coming from the half-dead tropical plants suspended from the wall, the limp foliage outstretched as if trying to reach Miranda on their last gasp.

Miranda slumped back on one of the wicker divans. Fruit spilled from a basket across a glass-topped table. She munched half a grape, peered critically at the pip, then waved Ransom in.

'Come on, doctor, don't stand there trying to look enigmatic. I won't compromise you or anything. Have you seen Quilter?'

'He's hunting your house-boy with a couple of dogs,' Ransom said. 'You may need me later. I'll be at home.' Miranda flicked the grape-skin across the floor. He tapped his valise. 'I've got to go.'

'Where?' She waved at him contemptuously. 'Don't be damn silly, there's nowhere to go. Tell me, doctor, what exactly are you up to in Hamilton?'

'Up to?' Ransom echoed. 'I'm trying to hold what's left of my practice together.'

As she poked among the half-eaten fruit Ransom looked down at the dirty cuffs and collar of the beach-robe, and at the soiled top of the slip she wore loosely around her breasts. Already she was beginning to look as derelict and faded as her plants – once she ceased to serve Lomax's purposes he would lose interest in her. Yet her skin was of an almost albino whiteness, unmarked by any freckle or blemish.

Miranda gave him an evil smirk, pushing back her hair with one wrist in a comically arch gesture. 'What's the matter, doctor? Do you want to examine me or something?'

'Most definitely not,' Ransom said evenly. He pointed to the tanker by the pool. The mechanic was winding the hose on to its winch. 'Is Lomax selling his water?'

'Like hell. I wanted him to pour it into the ground near the highway. Has Lomax told you about his plan? I suppose he couldn't contain himself with laughing like a small boy?'

'Do you mean his bonfire party? He invited me to take part.'

'Doctor, you should.' Miranda looked around with a flourish, the white hair veiling her face like a Medusa's crown. 'Let me tell you, though, I have a little plan of my own.'

'I'm sure you have,' Ransom said. 'But I'll be leaving for the coast soon.'

With a weary shake of the head, Miranda dismissed him. 'There isn't any coast now. There's only *here*, you'd better face that.' When he reached the door she called after him: 'Doctor, have you ever seen an army of ants try to cross a stream?'

From the steps Ransom looked out across the dusty roof-tops. The smoke pall hung over the distant city, but the air was brighter, reflected off the white ash that covered the river bed. The brief meeting with Miranda had unsettled him. At first he had felt sorry for the girl, but now he realized that, in her brother's phrase, she was coming into her own.

The mechanic opened the door of the tanker and climbed up into the cabin. He pulled a rifle from the locker behind the seat and propped it in the window. A small, stooped man with a patch over one eye, he glanced suspiciously at Ransom.

Ransom walked over to him. 'Are the army requisitioning water now?'

'This is a private gift.' The driver pointed up at Lomax's suite, as if unsure of his motives. 'For Mount Royal zoo.'

Ransom recognized the green overalls. 'Who's in charge now? Dr Barnes?'

'He's gone, flown like a bird. Only two of us left. Me and the Austen girl. That one's a worker.'

'Catherine Austen?' Ransom asked. 'Do you mean that some of the animals are still alive? I thought they'd all been destroyed.'

'What?' The driver rounded on him. 'Destroyed? Why?'

Surprised by his aggressive tone, Ransom said: 'Well, for their sake, if not for ours. This water won't last for ever.'

The driver leaned on the sill, pointing a reproving finger at Ransom. Although obviously not a man given to argument, he seemed to have been irritated by Ransom's remarks.

'They're all right,' he said. 'It doesn't have to last for ever.' He gestured at the dusty landscape around them. 'This is what they like. A few weeks from now and maybe we'll be able to let them *out*!'

He smiled at Ransom; his one eye gleamed in his twisted face with a wild misanthropic hope.

11

The Lamia

For half an hour they drove on towards Mount Royal zoo, winding in and out of the deserted streets, making detours across the gardens and tennis courts when their way was blocked. Ransom sat forward on the seat beside Whitman, trying to remember the maze of turnings. The zoo was three miles from the centre of the city, in what had once been a neighbourhood of pleasant, well-tended homes, but the area now had the appearance of a derelict shanty-town. The husks of trees and box hedges divided the houses from one another, and in the gardens the smouldering incinerators added their smoke to the ash-filled air. Abandoned cars lay by the roadside, or had been jerked out of the way on to the pavements, their doors open. They passed an empty shopping centre. The store fronts had been boarded up or sealed with steel grilles, and a few lean dogs with arched backs picked among the burst cartons.

The abrupt transition from Hamilton, which still carried a faint memory of normal life, surprised Ransom. Here, within the perimeter of the city, the exodus had been violent and sudden. Now and then a solitary figure hurried head down between the lines of cars. Once an ancient truck crammed with an entire family's furniture and possessions, parents crowded into the driving cabin with three or four children, jerked across an intersection a hundred yards in front of them and disappeared into the limbo of side-streets.

Half a mile from the zoo the main avenue was blocked by a dozen cars jammed around a large articulated truck that had tried to reverse into a narrow drive. Whitman swore and glanced briefly to left and right. Without hesitating he swung the tanker off the road into the drive of a small, single-storey house. They roared past the kitchen windows, crushing a dustbin with the fender, and Ransom saw the faces of a grey-haired old couple, a man and his wife, watching them with startled eyes.

'Did you see them?' Ransom shouted, casting his mind two or three weeks ahead, when the couple would be alone in the abandoned city. 'Is no one helping them?'

Whitman ignored the question. Ransom had persuaded the one-eyed driver, against his better judgment, to take him to the zoo on the pretext that he would be able to add an anti-rabies vaccine to the water. After his meeting with Lomax and Miranda the mention of Catherine Austen had cut across everything like a shaft of clear light, a small focus of sanity.

A white picket fence separated the end of the alley from the drive of the house on the parallel street. A car had stalled between the gates at the edge of the pavement. Barely reducing speed, Whitman drove on and flattened the fence. Carrying a section on the bumper, they moved past the house, then accelerated fractionally before the impact with the car. Doors slamming, it was catapulted out into the road, denting the grille of a small truck, then rolled across the camber and buried its bonnet in the side of an empty convertible. The windscreens frosted and windows splintered and fell into the roadway.

Somewhere a dog barked plaintively. His nostrils flicking at the sound, Whitman swung the tanker out on to the road, shedding the remains of the fence from the bumper. 'Can you see it? We can stop.'

'Not here – look out!' Ransom warned.

Fifty yards to their left two figures watched them from behind the corner of a house. Their black shawls, streaked with ash, covered their broad-cheeked faces, like the hoods of a primitive monastic order.

'Fishermen's wives,' Ransom said. 'They're coming down from the lake.'

'Forget them,' Whitman said. 'You can worry when they start moving in packs.'

Ransom sat back, knowing that even if this grim prospect were ever to materialize he himself would not be there. This change of heart had occurred after his visit to Lomax. There he had realized that the role of the recluse and solitary, meditating on his past sins of omission like a hermit on the fringes of an abandoned city, would not be viable. The blighted landscape and its empty violence, its loss of time, would provide its own motives.

These latent elements in Lomax and Miranda were already appearing. Curiously, Lomax was less frightening than Miranda. Her white hair and utter lack of pity reminded him of the spectre that appeared at all times of extreme exhaustion – the yellow-locked, leprous-skinned lamia who had pursued the Ancient Mariner. Perhaps this phantom embodied archaic memories of a time, whether past or future, when fear and pain were the most valuable emotions, and their exploitation into the most perverse forms the sole imperative.

It was this sense of remorseless caprice, with its world of infinite possibilities unrestrained by any moral consider-ations, which had its expression in the figure of the white-haired witch. As he watched the abandoned houses stretching along the ash-covered streets, and heard the restive cries of the animals as they skirted its wall, he saw an image of Miranda squatting in her filthy robe by some hearth among the smoking rubble, her perverted cherub's face like an old crone's.

Yet Lomax's references to the future, and his own confusion of the emerging landscape with the past, tantalized him. These last days in Hamilton had seemed to offer a choice of direction, but already he sensed that Lomax had been right. If the future, and his whole sense of time, were haunted by images of his own death, by the absence of identity beyond both birth and grave, why did these chimeras not coincide more closely with the terrifying vision of Miranda Lomax? He listened to the baying of the animals, raucous cries like tearing fabric, and thought to himself, they'll wake the dead.

12

The Drowned Aquarium

They approached the gates of the zoo. Whitman stopped the tanker at the metal barrier across the service entrance. Ransom climbed out and raised the boom, and Whitman drove the tanker to the pump-house behind the cages.

Ransom walked across the central promenade of the zoo. Some twenty pink flamingoes huddled together in a shallow trough at one end of the rock-pool, the water sunk to a pallid slush betwen their feet. Sheets of matting covered the wire mesh over the pool but the birds fretted nervously, opening their beaks at Ransom.

A monotonous chorus of bellows and grunts sounded around the zoo, the visceral cries reflected off the concrete pens. The smaller cages housing the ornamental birds and monkeys were empty. In one of the stalls a dead camel lay on the floor. Near by, a large Syrian bear prowled up and down its cage, arms and head rolling around the bars. A hyena stared at Ransom like a blind pig, emitting a high-pitched whine. Next to it a pair of cheetahs flicked around their cages, their small, killing heads swivelling as Ransom passed.

An attempt had been made to feed and water the animals. Clumps of monkey meat lay on the floors, and there were a few pails of water, but the cages were as dry as desert caves.

Ransom stopped in the entrance to the lion house. A

roar of noise greeted him, striking his head like a fist. The five white-haired lions – two pairs and a single older male – were about to be fed, and their roars sounded like the slamming of a steel mill. Striding up and down the narrow aisle between the rail and the bars was Catherine Austen. Her white shirt and riding breeches were stained with dirt and perspiration, but she moved without any sign of fatigue, hoisting a pail of meat under the noses of the lions as she tossed the giblets through the bars. At first Ransom thought she was tormenting them, but the lions bounded up and down, catching the meat in their jaws.

'Come on, Sarah, up, up! You're as slow as a cow! No, Hector, here!' At the end cage, where the single lion, a blind old male with a ragged mane and a dulled yellow hide, was swinging left and right like a demented bear, hoarse with bellowing, she heaped the meat through the bars almost into his jaws.

As the lions tore at the meat Catherine moved back along the cages, rattling her pail against the bars. Recognizing Ransom, she beckoned him towards her, then began to rake out the cages with a long-handled broom, tripping playfully at the lions' legs.

'Who's this?' she called over her shoulder. 'The veterinary?'

Ransom put his valise down on a bench. 'Your friend Whitman gave me a lift. He's brought Lomax's water.'

Catherine pulled her broom from the cage with a flourish. 'Good for him. I wasn't going to trust Lomax until I saw it come. Tell Whitman to pump it into the reserve tank.'

Ransom moved along the cages, the smell and energy of the lions quickening his blood. Catherine Austen had cast away all trace of lethargy and moodiness.

'I'm glad to see you, doctor. Have you come to help?'

Ransom took the broom from her and leaned it against the wall. 'In a sense.'

Catherine surveyed the floor, which was strewn with straw and splinters of bone. 'It may look a mess, but I think Father would have been proud of me.'

'Perhaps he would. How did you persuade Barnes to leave you here?'

'He worked for Father years ago. Whitman and I convinced him that we should stay on and put them down one at a time, so there wouldn't be any panic.'

'Are you going to?'

'What? Of course not. I know we can't hope to keep them all alive, but we'll try with the mammals. The lions we'll save right to the end.'

'And then?'

Catherine turned on him. 'What are you trying to say, doctor? I'd rather not think about it.'

Ransom stepped over to her. 'Catherine, be sensible for a moment. Lomax hasn't given this water to you out of charity – he obviously intends to use the animals for his own purposes. As for Whitman – perhaps zoos need people like him, but he's a menace on his own. It's time to leave, or one morning you'll come here and find all the cages open.'

Catherine wrenched her arm away from him. 'Doctor, can't you understand? It might *rain* tomorrow, much as you may hate the prospect. I don't intend to desert these animals, and as long as there's food and water I certainly can't destroy them.' Lowering her voice, she added: 'Besides, I don't think Whitman would let me.' She turned away and touched the cage of the blind lion.

'He probably wouldn't,' Ransom said. 'Remember, though, that here, unlike the world outside, you still have bars between you and the animals.'

Quietly, Catherine said: 'One day you're going to be surprised, doctor.'

Ransom was about to remonstrate with her again when

something moved behind him. Silhouetted against the sun-light was the faun-like figure that had already crept up behind him once that day.

Ransom stepped towards the door, but the youth darted away.

'What the devil is he up to? Has he been hanging around before?'

'Who was that? I didn't see him.'

'Lomax's familiar – Quilter.' A few feet from Ransom the lions munched at the joint of meat, jaws tearing through the bony shafts. Quilter's appearance had abruptly let another dimension into the already uncertain future of the zoo.

Hands in pockets, Catherine followed him into the sun-light. 'Tomorrow I'm moving in here, so I won't see you again, doctor. By the way, your houseboat hardly looks as if it's going anywhere.'

'I intend to put a stronger motor on it.' The sky was still stained by the plumes of smoke billowing upwards from the city. He saw Quilter moving past the entrance to the aviary, a circular wire-topped building that backed on to the pump-house.

Catherine slipped her arm through his. 'Why don't you join me, doctor? We'll teach the lions to hunt in packs.'

She waved and walked away among the cages.

Clasping the valise, Ransom set off across the central promenade. He stopped behind the flamingo pool. Around him the animals patrolled their cages in the bright sun. The water tanker stood by the pump-house, its hose trailing into a manifold. Whitman had gone off to the living quar-ters near the gates.

A bird's cry pierced the air, ending in a flat squawk. Ransom walked along the wall of the pool, searching the empty passages between the cages. He stepped out into the open and moved towards the pump-house, hiding in the shade below the roofs of the cages. The bear swayed along the bars after him, trying to embrace him in its ponderous arms. The cheetahs' tails flicked like whips, their cold eyes cutting at Ransom.

He stepped into the entrance to the aquarium. Faint sunlight filtered through the matting laid on the frosted glass overhead, a crack here and there illuminating a corner of one of the tanks. The usual liquid glimmer had been stilled, and there was a sharp tang in the air. Ransom moved between the lines of tanks towards the service door beyond the alligator pit, then paused as his eyes cleared in the darkness.

Suspended in the dim air around him, their pearly bodies rotating like the vanes of elaborate mobiles, were the corpses of hundreds of fish. Poisoned by their own wastes, they hung in the gloomy water, their blank eyes glowing like phosphorus, mouths agape. In the smaller tanks the tropical fish effloresced like putrid jewels, their coloured tissue dissolving into threads of gossamer. Gazing at them, Ransom had a sudden vision of the sea by the coastal beaches, as clouded and corpse-strewn as the water in the tanks, the faces of the drowned eddying past each other.

He crossed the aquarium and stepped into the service unit. A narrow yard led him into the rear of the pump-house. The machinery was silent, the large flywheel stationary in its pit. Masking his footsteps, he approached the open double doors, through which he could see the green hull of the water-tanker.

Standing with his back to Ransom as he examined the damp hose leading into the manifold, was Quilter. He wore the same filthy trousers stained with wine and grease, but he now sported an expensive gold-and-purple Paisley shirt. Suspended from his belt by a piece of string fastened around its severed neck was a dead peacock, its jewelled tail sweeping behind him like a train.

A fly circled the air above his head, then alighted on his neck. Absent-mindedly, Quilter raised one hand and slapped the insect into a red smudge. He picked thoughtfully at the remains.

Ransom stepped out into the sunlight. With his right hand he held Quilter's arm above the elbow.

Startled, Quilter looked around, his liquid eyes rolling beneath his dented brows.

'Doctor —'

'Hello, Quilter.' Gripping the muscular biceps, an immense bulge of muscle, Ransom glanced between the wheels of the tanker for any signs of the Alsatians. 'Is this your afternoon off? I didn't know you enjoyed zoos.'

'Doctor . . .' Quilter gazed down at the fingers clenched around his arm, a puzzled frown on his face. 'Doctor, I don't like —' He jerked his arm away, then lashed out at Ransom with the edge of his hand. Ready for this, Ransom side-stepped, knocking Quilter off-balance with his elbow, and clouted him across the shoulders with the valise. Quilter sat down on the concrete, the peacock's tail flaring between his legs. For a moment he seemed stunned. Then a rheumy smile struggled fitfully on to his deformed face.

His point made, Ransom leaned against the side of the tanker, washing his hand in the water dribbling from the hose.

'You should be more careful, Quilter. Now what are you up to here?'

Quilter shook his head, apparently mystified by Ransom's behaviour. He pointed to the water on Ransom's fingers. 'One day, doctor, you'll drown in that much water.'

'Keep to the point. What are you doing so far from home?'

Quilter gazed at him guilelessly. He stood up, hitching the peacock on to his hip, then inspected his shirt with

great care. 'Lomax told me to follow you; tell him everything you did.'

'Interesting.' Ransom pondered this. The frankness
could be discounted. No doubt these were Lomax's instruc-
tions, but the real point of Quilter's remark would lie elsewhere. 'As a matter of fact Lomax invited me to stay with
him,' he said, adding with deliberate irony: 'You'll be
working for me then, Quilter.'

Quilter regarded him sceptically, his toad's face full of
bile. 'I'm working for Miss Miranda,' he said.

'*That* makes more sense.' Ransom watched Quilter's face
as it started to quiver, breaking into a mirthless laugh.
The scarred lips shook silently, the mole on his left cheek
dancing. Repelled by this grimacing parody of a human
being, Ransom turned to go, hoping to draw Quilter away
from Catherine Austen and the zoo. As long as the animals
were alive Whitman would guard her, but the one-eyed
man would be no match for Quilter.

'I wish you both luck,' he called back over his shoulder.
'You have a lot in common.'

Quilter stared after him, his eyes suddenly glazed,
fingers feeling the blood-streaked neck of the peacock
hanging from his belt. Then, with virulent energy he
hurled after Ransom: 'We'll have more in common later,
doctor! Much more!'

13

The Nets

Outside the zoo, Ransom waited before crossing the street. He rested against the trunk of a dead plane tree, watching the deserted houses. Quilter's absurd words, crazier than even he could understand, echoed in Ransom's ears. Normally the youth would have tittered at the grotesque implications of the remark, but his obvious conviction in this new realm of possibility made Ransom suspect that he was at last out of his depth. Perhaps the boy was regaining his sanity – no lunatic would ever dream up such an implausible fantasy.

Retracing the route Whitman had taken, Ransom set off across the street. The houses were empty, the garbage fires drifting from the gardens. The city was silent and the billows of the burning oil fires still rose into the air over his head. A door swung open, reflecting the sun with a sharp stab. Somewhere to his left there was a clatter as a lost dog overturned a refuse bin.

Barely filtered by the smoke, the sunlight burned across the ashy dust, the flints of quartz stinging his eyes. After walking for a quarter of an hour Ransom regretted not bringing a flask of water. The dust filled his throat with the dry taste of burning garbage. Leaning on the fender of a car, he massaged his neck, and debated whether to break into one of the houses.

A short way ahead he passed an open front door. Pushing

back the gate, he walked up the path to the porch. Hidden by the shade, he glanced up and down the empty street. Through the door he could see into the living-room and kitchen. Cardboard cartons were stacked in the hall, and unwanted suitcases lay across the armchairs.

He was about to step through the door when he noticed a small sign drawn in the dust a few feet away from him. The single loop, like a child's caricature of a fish, had been casually traced with a stick lying on the path near by.

Ransom watched the houses around him. The sign had been made within the last minutes, but the street was silent. He walked off down the path. His first reaction was to blame Quilter for the sign, but he then remembered the two fishermen's women in black shawls whom he had seen from the tanker, and the strange congregation at the church that morning. The sign outside the church had been the same simple loop, by coincidence the rebus used by the first Christians to identify themselves to one another. The fishermen's sullen expressions as they listened to the Reverend Johnstone's sermon on Jonah and the gourd were probably in many ways like those on the obsessed faces of the primitive fishermen who left their nets by the Lake of Galilee.

A hundred yards away a black-suited figure moved behind a wall. Ransom stopped, waiting for the man to come out into the road. Quickening his pace, he set off along the avenue again, ignoring a door that opened behind him. Deliberately avoiding the route he and Whitman had taken, he turned left at the first intersection, then right again into the next street. Behind him, the ash drifted down across the roads, lightly covering the foot-prints.

Five minutes later he could hear all around him the running steps of the men following his path. Hidden behind the intervening walls and houses, they moved along with him, extending in two arcs on either side, like a group of small boats tracking a sounding whale. The muffled footsteps padded across the empty porches. Ransom crouched down and rested between two cars. Behind him the smoke plumes rising from the gardens were disturbed and broken.

He strode on again, pausing only at the crossroads. Despite his progress, Hamilton still seemed to lie a mile or so beyond the roof-tops, as if his invisible pursuers were steering him in a circle. Wondering why they should bother to follow him, he remembered Catherine Austen's jibe – perhaps the fishermen marooned ashore by the dying lake were hunting for some kind of scapegoat?

He slowed down to regain his breath, and then made a last effort. He broke into a run and turned left and right at random, darting in and out of the cars. To his relief his pursuers seemed to drop behind. He turned again into the next street, and then found that he had blundered into a cul-de-sac.

Retracing his steps, Ransom saw two black-suited figures scuttle through a gap in a ruined wall. He raced along the white dust covering the pavement, but the road was full of running men, vaulting across the cars like acrobats. A large net lay over the pavement. As he approached, it rose into the air, cast at him off the ground. Ransom turned and clambered between two cars. In the centre of the road half a dozen men appeared around him, arms outstretched as they feinted with their nets, watching his feet with intent eyes. Their black serge suits were streaked with ash.

Ransom tried to break through them, using his weight to shoulder two of the men aside. The heavy shawl of a net was thrown over his face. Knocking it away with the valise, he tripped in the tarry skeins underfoot, cast at him like lassos from all directions. As he fell the fishermen closed around him, and the nets caught him before he could touch the ground. Swept off his feet, he was tumbled on to his back in the huge hammock, then lifted into the air on a dozen arms as if he were about to be tossed to the sun. Pulling at the thick mesh, he shouted at the men, and caught a last confused glimpse of their pointed faces below their caps. There was a wild scramble across the road, and his shoulders struck the ground. Swept up again, he collided head-on with the fender of a car.

14

A New River

Illuminated by the tinted sky, the curved beams rose above
Ransom on either side, reaching inwards to the open space
over his head like the ribs of a stranded whale. Lying back
on an old mattress, Ransom counted the girders, for a
moment imagining that he was indeed lying within the
bowels of a beached leviathan, its half-rotten carcass forgotten on the shore.

Between the beams the lower hull-plates were intact,
and walled him into the hold. Beyond his feet was the
prow of the ship, one of the old herring-trawlers in the
breakers' yards somewhere along the river towards Mount
Royal. Metal ladders reached up the outer sides of the hull,
and the floor was covered with piles of metal sheeting,
port-holes and sections of bulkhead. In the turning afternoon light the mournful wreck was filled by a last fleeting
glow.

Ransom sat up on one elbow, feeling the grazes on his
cheeks and forehead. One of the lapels had been almost torn
from his linen jacket, and he pulled this off and pressed the
pad to his temple. He remembered the nets closing around
him in the hot airless road, like the capes of bull-fighters
called out to the streets behind their arena to play a huge
fish found leaping in the dust. He had been carried half-
conscious to the docks and tipped into the trawler's hold.
Through a gap in the port side of the hull he could see

the roof of a warehouse, a collection of gantries leaning against it. The smells of paint and tar drifted across the air.

Behind him the stern bridge of the trawler reached into the sky. Two life-belts hung like punctured eyes from the rail on either side of the bridge-house. Below, a faint light came from one of the cabins. There were no sounds of the fishermen, but a single figure patrolled the deck, a metal gaff in one hand.

Ransom pulled himself on to his knees. He wiped his hands on the tags of cloth sticking from the mattress. The trawler had been beached in an undredged dock below the former river level, and the wet mud had seeped through the keel plates. The dark cakes lay around him like lumps of damp lava. He stood up, his head drumming from the mild concussion, and groped across the floor of the hold. He paused behind the mast-brace, listening to a vague noise from the streets ashore. Then he felt his way down the starboard side of the hull, searching for a loose plate. On the bridge, the look-out patrolled the stern, watching the smoke-fires burning in the city.

The noise drew nearer, the sounds of men running. Ransom went back to the mattress and lay down. The footsteps raced past the warehouse, and the group of ten or so fishermen reached the wharf and crossed the wooden gangway to the bridge deck. Between them they carried a large bundle in their nets. They leaned over the rail and lowered it down into the hold, steering it over the mattress. Then they released the nets and tipped a half-unconscious man on to the mattress beside Ransom.

The bos'un in charge of the hunting party came to the rail and peered down at this latest catch. A stocky, broad-shouldered man of about thirty, he was distinguished from the others by a mop of blond hair over his plump face. Ransom let his jaw hang slackly and fixed his eyes on one of the beams. Two feet from him the new arrival, a grey-haired tramp in an old overcoat, snuffled and coughed, moaning to himself.

The blond man nodded to his men. They hauled up their nets and slung them over their shoulders.

A door opened in the bridge-house, revealing the light of a lantern. A tall man with a dark wasted face stepped out on to the deck, looking around him with a strong gaze. His black suit was buttoned to the neck, emphasizing the length of his arms and chest.

'Jonas—!' The bo'sun strode across the deck and tried to close the door.

'Don't fear the light, Saul.' The tall man pushed his arm away. After a pause he shut the door, then moved forward among his men. He nodded to each of them in turn, as if approving their presence on his quarter-deck. In turn they glanced up at him with deferential nods, fingering the nets on their shoulders as if aware that they should be about some useful task. Only the blond-haired Saul seemed to resent his authority. He hung about irritably behind Jonas, tapping the rail as if looking for something to complain about.

Jonas crossed the bridge and stood by the fore-rail. His slow movements along the deck had a kind of deliberate authority, as if this were the largest vessel he had ever commanded and he was carefully measuring himself against it, taking no chances that a sudden swell might topple him from his bridge. His face had the hardness of beaten leather, drained of all moisture by sun and wind. As he looked into the hold, his long arms reaching to the rail, Ransom recognized the marked slope of his forehead and the sharp arrow-like cheekbones. His eyes had the over-intense but alert look of a half-educated migrant preacher constantly distracted by the need to find food and shelter.

He nodded at the supine figures of Ransom and the

drunken tramp. 'Good. Two more to join us in the search. Now back to your nets and sweep the streets. There'll be good catches for the next two nights.'

The men clambered to their feet, but the bo'sun shouted: 'Jonas! We don't need the old men now!' He waved contemptuously at the hold. 'They be dead bait, they'll weigh us down!' He launched into a half-coherent tirade, to which Jonas listened with head bowed, as if trying to control some inner compulsive nervousness. The men sat down again, grumbling to each other, some agreeing with Saul's complaints with forceful nods, others shifting about uncertainly. The loyalties of the group swerved from one man to the other, held together only by the unstated elements which they all sensed in Jonas's isolated figure.

'Saul!' The tall captain silenced him. He had long hands which he used like an actor. Watching him, Ransom noticed the calculation in all his movements as he stepped about on the high stage of the bridge. 'Saul, we reject no one. They need our help now. Remember, there is nothing here.'

'But, Jonas—!'

'Saul!'

The blond bo'sun gave up, nodding to himself with a tic-like jerk. As the men shuffled along the deck to the gangway he gave Jonas a bitter backward glance.

Left alone, Jonas gazed across the darkening streets. As the men went off, nets over their shoulders, he watched them with the narrow compassion of a man born into a hard and restricted world. He paced the bridge of his skeleton ship, looking up at the smoke billows rising from the city, as if debating whether to trim his sails before a storm.

The old tramp moaned on the mattress beside Ransom, blood running from one ear. His overcoat was stained by a pink fluid that Ransom guessed to be anti-freeze. Now and then he woke for a lucid interval, and then sank off again, gazing at the sky with wild sad eyes.

Ransom stood up and groped across the hold. Above him Jonas came to the rail and beckoned him forward, smiling at Ransom as if he had been waiting for him to wake. He called to the look-out, and a ladder was lowered into the hold.

Painfully, Ransom managed to climb halfway to the rail, and Jonas's strong hands reached down and seized his arms. He lifted Ransom on to the deck, then pressed him to sit down.

Ransom pointed to the tramp. 'He's injured. Can you bring him up here? I'm a doctor, I'll do what I can.'

'Of course.' Jonas waved a long arm at the look-out. 'Go down and we'll lift him out.' As he held the ladder he said to Ransom: 'A doctor, good. You'll come with us, we need everyone we can find for the search.'

Ransom leaned on the rail, feeling his head clear. 'Search for where? What are you looking for?'

'For a new river.' Jonas gestured with a sweep of his long arms, encompassing the fading skyline and half the land. 'Somewhere there. My bos'un tells them to laugh at me, but I have *seen* it!' He seemed to half-believe his own boast.

The sounds of running feet came from the distant streets. Ransom listened to them approach. He waited as the look-out climbed down into the hold, a net over one shoulder. Within a minute any chance of escape would have gone. Ten feet away was the gangway. Beside the warehouse a small alley led away into the near-by streets.

Jonas leaned over the rail, his body bent at the waist like a gallows. The tramp lay slackly in the cradle of the net, and Jonas's powerful arms lifted him into the air, like a fisherman hauling in an immense catch.

Ransom stood up, as if offering to help, then turned and ran for the gangway. When the boards sprang below his feet Jonas turned and cried out, as if trying to warn him of his error, but Ransom was across the wharf and racing up the alley.

Behind the warehouse he saw the fishermen coming down the street, a man struggling in the outstretched nets. At their head was the blond-haired bo'sun. He saw Ransom and broke into a run, his short arms hooking in front of him.

Ransom ran past the houses, but within thirty yards Saul was at his shoulder, his feet kicking at Ransom's as they swerved in and out of the cars.

Suddenly two whirling forms leapt from behind a wall, and with a flash of teeth hurled themselves on the bo'sun. Out of breath, Ransom ran forward for another fifty yards, then stopped behind a car as the two Alsatians snarled and jumped at Saul's head, tearing at his swinging fists.

'Doctor! This way!'

Ransom turned to see the bright-shirted figure of Quilter, the peacock hanging from his waist, waving at him farther along the road. Leaving the dogs, Ransom limped forward after the youth as he ran on, the tail speckling at his heels.

Lost in a maze of dusty streets, he followed Quilter across the fences and gardens, sometimes losing sight of him as he leapt through the smoke of the refuse fires. Once, searching about in a walled garden into which he had blundered, Ransom found the youth gazing down at the half-burned carcass of a large dog lying across a heap of embers, his face staring at it with child-like seriousness.

Finally they stepped over a low parapet on to the bank of the river. A mile away to their left was the span of the motor-bridge. Below them, across the white bed of the channel, Philip Jordan stood in the stern of his skiff, leaning on his pole. Quilter strode down the bank, sinking to his knees through the dry crust, the peacock's tail brushing the dust up into Ransom's face.

Ransom followed him down the slope, pausing by a stranded lighter. The sun was half-hidden by the western horizon. The smoke plumes overhead were darker and more numerous, but the basin of the river gleamed with an almost spectral whiteness.

'Come on, doctor! You can rest later.'

Surprised by this brusque call, Ransom looked round at Philip Jordan, uneasy at this association between Quilter, the grotesque Caliban of all his nightmares, and the calm-eyed Ariel of the river. He walked down to the skiff, his feet sinking in the damper mud by the water's edge. As the evening light began to fade the burnt yellow of the old lion's skin shone in Philip Jordan's arrow-like face. Impatient to leave, he watched Ransom with remote eyes.

Quilter sat alone in the stern, a water-borne Buddha, the shadows of the oily surface mottling his face. As Ransom stepped aboard he let out two piercing whistles. They echoed away across the bank, reflected off the concrete parapet. One of the dogs appeared. Tail high, it sprang down on to the bank, in a flurry of dust raced to the skiff, and leapt aboard over Ransom's shoulder. Settling itself between Quilter's feet, it whined at the dusk. Quilter waited, watching the parapet. A frown crossed his face. The Alsatian whined again. Quilter nodded to Philip Jordan, and the craft surged away across the darkening mirror of the surface, the peacock's tail sweeping above the water like a jewelled sail.

Four miles away, the intervals in its skyline closed by the dusk, the dark bulk of Mount Royal rose below the smoke plumes like a sombre volcano.

15

The Burning Altar

The next morning, after a night of uproar and violence, Ransom began his preparations for departure.

Shortly before dawn, when the sounds of gunfire at last subsided, he fell asleep, on the settee in the sitting-room, the embers of the burnt-out house across the avenue lifting into the air like clouds of fireflies. He had reached home at seven o'clock, exhausted after his escape from Jonas and the fishermen. The lakeside town was quiet, a few torches glowing as the Reverend Johnstone's militia patrolled the darkened street, methodically closing the doors of the abandoned cars and putting out the refuse fires in the gardens. Only Lomax's house showed any lights from its windows.

After taking off his suit, Ransom had filled the bath, then knelt over the edge and drank slowly from his hands, massaging his face and neck with the tepid water. He thought of Philip Jordan, swinging the long prow of the skiff between the stranded hulks, the reflection of his narrow face carried away in the dark water like the ghosts of all the other illusions that had sustained Ransom during the previous weeks. The unspoken link between Philip Jordan and the ambiguous figure of Quilter, brooding over his lost dog as he fingered the luminous fan of the peacock's tail, seemed to exclude him from Hamilton even more than the approaching fishermen with their quest for a lost river. All this made him wonder what his own role might become, and the real nature of the return of the desert to the land. As Ransom stepped from the boat he had tried to speak to Philip, but the youth avoided his eyes. With a guttural noise in his throat he had leaned on his pole and pivoted the boat away into the darkness, leaving Ransom with the last image of Quilter smiling at him like a white idol, his ironic farewell drifting across the oily water.

For an hour Ransom lay in the bath, resolving to leave as soon as he had recovered. Somehow he would persuade Catherine Austen to join him – the landscape around them was no longer a place for the sane. Soothed by the warm water, he was almost asleep when there was a muffled explosion in the distance, and an immense geyser of flame shot up into the night sky. The shaft of glowing air illuminated the tiles in the darkened bathroom as he climbed from the water. For five minutes he watched the fire burning strongly like a discharging furnace. As it subsided the softer light reflected the outbuildings of a small paint factory half a mile from the zoo.

An unsettled silence followed. Dressing himself in a clean suit, Ransom watched from the window. The Reverend Johnstone's house remained quiet, but Lomax's mansion was a hive of activity. Lights flared in the windows and moved up and down the verandas. Someone carried a huge multiple-armed candlestick on to the roof and lifted it high into the air as if inspecting the stars. Torches flickered across the lawn. More and more oil-lamps were lit, until the white rotunda of the house seemed to be bathed by rows of spotlights.

Ransom was preparing a small meal for himself in the kitchen when a brilliant firework display began in Lomax's garden. A score of rockets rose over the house and exploded into coloured umbrellas, catherine wheels span, bursting into cascades of sparks. Roman candles tied to the trees around the garden poured a pink mushy light into the darkness, setting fire to part of the hedge. In the swerving light Ransom could see the white figures of Lomax and his sister moving about on the roof.

After the initial crescendo, the display continued for ten minutes, the rockets falling away into the darkness towards the city. Whatever Lomax's motives, the timing and extravagance of the show convinced Ransom that he was trying to draw attention to himself, that the display was a challenge to those still hiding in the deserted outskirts of the city.

Listening to the rockets explode and fall, their harsh sighs carried away over the roof-tops, Ransom noticed that the reports were louder, mingled with hard cracking detonations that rocked the windows with the impact of real explosives. Immediately the firework display ended, and the lights in Lomax's house were smothered. A few canisters burned themselves out on the lawn.

The whine and crack of the gunfire continued. The shots approached Hamilton, coming at ten-second intervals, as if a single weapon were being used. Ransom went out into the drive. A bullet whipped fifty feet overhead with a thin whoop, lost across the river. The Reverend Johnstone's jeep sped past down the avenue, its lights out, then stopped at the first corner. Three men jumped down and ran between the trees towards the church.

Five minutes later, as he followed them down the road, Ransom could hear the organ above the gunfire. The faint chorale droned and echoed, the ragged, uneven sounds suggesting that someone other than the Reverend Johnstone was at the keyboard. Ransom crouched behind the trees, watching two of Johnstone's men firing at the porch of the church from behind an overturned car. As they were driven back, Ransom crossed the road and hid himself in one of the empty houses. The organ continued to play above the sporadic gunfire, and Ransom saw the blond-haired Saul, rifle in hand, hanging back as he beckoned his men between the cars. Apart from Saul, none of the fishermen was armed, and they carried staves torn from the fences along the pavement.

Ransom waited until they had moved past, and then worked his way between the houses. He slipped through the narrow alleys behind the garages, climbing in and out of open windows until he reached the house facing the church. From the edge of the road he could see through the open doors. The music had stopped and the tall figure of Jonas swayed from the pulpit, his long arms gesturing to the three men hunched together in the front pew. In the light of the single oil-lamp his face flickered as if in high fever, his hoarse voice trying to shout down the gunfire in the streets.

One of the men stood up and left him, and Ransom saw the spire of the church illuminated against the night sky. Smoke raced along the eaves, and then the flames furled themselves round the tower. Jonas looked up, halted in the middle of his sermon. His hands clutched at the flames racing among the vaulting. The two men turned and ran out, ducking their heads below the smoke.

Ransom left the house and crossed the road. The fire burned along the length of the nave, and already the smaller roofing timbers were falling on to the pews. As he ran down the path to the vestry door the blond-haired bo'sun darted from the aisle. His face and chest were lit by the flames as he stopped in the centre of the road to look back at the church. In his hand he carried the broken shaft of a wooden gaff.

Shielding his head, Ransom stepped through the chancel. In the nave the falls of red-hot charcoal were setting fire to the prayer books in the pews. Burning petrol covered the lectern and altar, and flared from a pool around the base of the pulpit.

Slumped inside the pulpit was the broken figure of Jonas, his arms and legs sticking out loosely. Propped on to his temples was a strange head-piece, the severed head of a huge fish taken from the tank of dead sturgeons at the zoo. As Ransom pulled Jonas from the burning pulpit the fish's head, a grotesque silver mitre, toppled forwards into his arms. Embedded between his eyes was the metal barb of the gaff Ransom had seen in the bo'sun's hand outside the church.

Ransom dragged the barely conscious man through the vestry and out into the cool air of the churchyard. He laid him down among the gravestones and wiped the fish's blood off his bruised forehead. Jonas stirred, his chest moving again. Suddenly he started upright from the grave. His long hand grasped Ransom's arm. His mouth worked in a silent gabble, as if discharging the whole of his sermon, his eyes staring at Ransom in the light of the consumed church.

Then he subsided into a deep sleep, his lungs seizing at the air. As his men returned along the street Ransom left him and slipped away into the darkness.

For the next hour, as Ransom watched from an upstairs window, gunfire sounded intermittently through the streets. At times it would retreat between the houses, then come back almost to his doorstep. Once there were shouts in the avenue, and Ransom saw a man with a rifle running by at full speed, and a group of men in front of the Reverend Johnstone's house driving cars up on to the pavement to form a barricade. Then the noise subsided again.

It was during one of these intermissions, when Ransom went downstairs to sleep, that the two houses across the road were set on fire. The light illuminated the whole avenue, and flared through the windows of the lounge, throwing Ransom's shadow on to the wall behind him.

Two of Johnstone's men approached as the flames burned through the roofs, and then backed away from the heat.

From the window, Ransom caught a glimpse in the brilliant light of a squat, hunch-backed figure standing at the edge of the lawn between the houses, almost within the circle of flames. Pacing up and down beside it was a lithe cat-like creature on a leash, with a small darting head and the movements of a nervous whip.

16

The Terminal Zone

At noon, when Ransom woke, he heard the sounds of two army trucks farther down the road. The streets were deserted again. Diagonally across the avenue were the remains of two houses burned down during the night, the charred roof-beams jutting from the walls. Exhausted by the previous day, Ransom lay on the settee, listening to the trucks reverse and park. Even these distant sounds brought with them a threat of aimless violence, as if the whole landscape were about to fall apart again. Rallying himself with an effort, Ransom went into the kitchen and made himself some coffee. He leaned on the taps as the water leaked slowly into the percolator, and looked through the window at the embers still smoking on the ground, wondering how long it would be before his own house caught fire.

When he went out five minutes later one of the trucks was standing outside the Reverend Johnstone's drive. Hamilton was now a terminal zone, its deserted watch-towers and roof-tops turning white under the cloudless sky. The lines of cars, some with their windows smashed, lay along both sides of the road, covered by the ash settling from the refuse fires. The dried trees and hedges splintered in the hot sky. The smoke from the city was heavier, and a dozen plumes rose into the air.

The truck by the minister's house was loaded to its roof

with camping equipment and crates of supplies. A shot-gun rested on the seats by the tail-board. Edward Gunn, the owner of the hardware store and Johnstone's senior verger, knelt by the rear bumper, shackling on a small two-wheeled water trailer. He nodded at Ransom and picked up the shot-gun, pocketing his keys as he walked back to the drive.

'There goes another one.' He pointed into the haze towards the city. Billows of white smoke mushroomed over the roofs, followed by tips of eager flame, almost colourless in the hot sunlight. There was no sound, but to Ransom the burning house seemed only a few hundred yards away.

'Are you leaving?' Ransom asked.

Gunn nodded. 'You'd better come too, doctor.' His beaked face was thin and grey, like a tired bird's. 'There's nothing to stay for now. Last night they burned down the church.'

'I saw that,' Ransom said. 'Some kind of madness was running through the fishermen. Perhaps it was an accident.'

'No, doctor. They heard the minister's sermon yesterday. *That's* all they left for us.' He indicated the second truck being made ready for departure farther up the drive. Behind it a large motor-launch sat on a trailer. Fastened amidships was the battered frame of the Reverend Johnstone's pulpit, its charred rail rising into the air like the launch's bridge. Frances and Vanessa Johnstone, the minister's younger daughters, stood beside it.

Their father emerged from the house, a clean surplice over one arm. He wore knee-length rubber boots and a tweed fishing jacket with elbow patches. Climbing up into the pulpit on the launch, he looked as if he were about to set off on an arduous missionary expedition through some river-infested wilderness. Over his shoulder he bellowed: 'All right, everybody! All aboard!'

Julia, the eldest of the three daughters, stepped up behind Ransom. 'Father's becoming the old sea-dog already.' She took Ransom's arm, smiling at him with her grey eyes. 'What about you, Charles? Are you coming with us? Father,' she called out, 'don't you think we should have a ship's doctor with us?'

Preoccupied, Johnstone climbed down from the launch and went off indoors. 'Sybil, time to go!' Standing in the hall, he gazed around the house, at the shrouded furniture and the books stacked on the floor. An expression of numbness and uncertainty came over his strong face. Then he murmured something to himself and seemed to rally.

Ransom waited by the launch, Julia's hand still on his arm. Vanessa Johnstone was watching him with distant eyes, her pale hands hidden in the pockets of her slacks. Despite the sunlight on her face, her skin remained as white as it had been during the most critical days of her long illness four years earlier. She wore her black hair undressed to her shoulders, the single parting emphasizing the oval symmetry of her face. The metal support on her right leg was hidden by her slacks.

Looking at her for this last moment, Ransom was aware of the unstated links between himself and this crippled young woman. The blanched features of her face, from which pain and memories alike had been washed away, as if all time had been drained from them, seemed to Ransom like an image from his own future. For Vanessa, like himself, the past no longer existed. From now on they would both have to create their own sense of time out of the landscape emerging around them.

Ransom helped her over the tailboard of the truck.

'Goodbye, Charles,' she said. 'I hope everything is all right with you.'

'Don't write me off yet. I'll be following you down there.'

'Of course.' Vanessa settled herself. 'I saw you out on the lake the other day.'

'It's almost gone. I wish you could have come with me, Vanessa.'

'Perhaps I will one day. Take Philip Jordan with you when you go, Charles. He won't understand that he can't stay.'

'If he'll come. By the way, do you know the captain of the fishermen – Jonas, his name is . . .'

Gunn and his wife made their way down the drive, carrying a wicker hamper between them. The party began to move off. Leaving Vanessa, Ransom said goodbye to Sybil Johnstone, and then went over to the front door, where the clergyman was searching for his keys.

'Wish us luck, Charles.' He locked the door and walked with Ransom to the launch. 'Do watch that fellow Lomax.'

'I will. I'm sorry about the church.'

'Not at all.' Johnstone shook his head vigorously, his eyes strong again. 'It was painful, Charles, but necessary. Don't blame those men. They did exactly as I bade them – "God prepared a worm and it smote the gourd." '

He looked up at the charred pulpit, and then at the drained white basin of the river, winding towards the city and the distant smoke clouds. The wind had turned, and carried the plumes towards the north, the collapsing ciphers leaning against the sky.

'Which way are you going?' Ransom asked.

'South, to the coast.' Johnstone patted the bows of the launch. 'You know, I sometimes think we ought to accept the challenge and set off north, right into the centre of the drought . . . There's probably a great river waiting for us somewhere there, brown water and green lands—'

17

The Cheetah

Ransom watched from the centre of the road as they set off a few minutes later, the women waving from the tailboard. The small convoy, the launch and water trailer in tow, moved between the lines of cars, then turned at the first intersection and laboured away past the ruined church.

Left alone, Ransom listened to the fading sounds occasionally carried across to him as the trucks stopped at a road junction. The refuse fires drifted over the avenue, but otherwise the whole of Hamilton was silent, the sunlight reflected off the falling flakes of ash. Looking down the rows of vehicles, Ransom realized that he was now effectively alone in Hamilton, as he had unconsciously intended from the beginning.

He walked forward along the centre of the road, letting his feet fall into the steps printed into the ash in front of him. Somewhere a window broke. Hesitating to move from his exposed position, Ransom stopped, estimating that the sound came from two or three hundred yards away.

Behind him, he heard a thin spitting noise. Ransom looked around. Involuntarily he stepped back across the road. Ten feet away, watching him with the small precise gaze of a moody jeweller, a fully grown cheetah stood on the edge of the kerb. It moved forward, its claws extending as it felt delicately for the roadway.

'Doctor . . .' Partly hidden behind one of the trees, Quilter sprang lightly on his left foot, holding the steel leash attached to the cheetah's collar. He watched Ransom with a kind of amiable patience, stroking the fleece-lined jacket he wore over his shirt. His pose of vague disinterest in his surroundings implied that he now had all the time in the world. In a sense, Ransom realized, this was literally true.

'What do you want?' Ransom kept his voice level. The cheetah advanced on to the roadway and crouched down on its haunches, eyeing Ransom. Well within its spring, Ransom stared back at it, wondering what game Quilter was playing with this silent feline killer. 'I'm busy, Quilter. I can't waste any more time.'

He made an effort to turn. The cheetah flicked an eye at him, like a referee noticing an almost imperceptible infringement of the rules.

'Doctor . . .' With a smile, as if decanting a pearl from his palm, Quilter let the leash slide off his hand into the road.

'Quilter, you bloody fool—!' Controlling his temper, Ransom searched for something to say. 'How's your mother these days, Quilter? I've been meaning to call and see her.'

'Mother?' Quilter peered at Ransom. Then he tittered to himself, amused by this appeal to old sentiments. 'Doctor, not now . . .'

He picked up the leash and jerked the cat backwards with a brisk wrench. 'Come on,' he said to Ransom, prepared to forgive him this gaffe. 'Miss Miranda wants to see you.'

Ransom followed him through the gateway. The garden was littered with burnt-out canisters and the wire skeletons of catherine wheels. Several rockets had exploded against the house, and the black flashes disfigured the white paint.

'My dear Charles . . .' The plump figure of Richard

Lomax greeted Ransom on the steps. He had exchanged his white suit for another of even more brilliant luminosity. As he raised his little arms in greeting the silk folds ran like liquid silver. His pomaded hair and cherubic face, and the two jewelled clasps pinning his tie inside his double-breasted waistcoat, made him look like some kind of hallucinatory clown, the master of ceremonies at a lunatic carnival. Although Ransom was a dozen steps from him he raised his pudgy hands to embrace him reassuringly. 'My dear Charles, they've left you.'

'The Johnstones?' Ransom rested a foot on the lowest step. Behind him Quilter released the cheetah. It bounded away across the ashy surface of the lawn. 'They were quite right to leave. There's nothing to stay for here.'

'Rubbish!' Lomax beckoned him forward with a crooked finger. 'Charles, you look worried about something. You're not yourself today. Didn't you enjoy my firework display last night?'

'Not altogether, Richard. I'm leaving this afternoon.'

'But, Charles —' With an expansive shrug Lomax gave up the attempt to dissuade him, then flashed his most winning smile. 'Very well, if you must take part in this madness. Miranda and I have all sorts of things planned. And Quilter's having the time of his life.'

'So I've noticed,' Ransom commented. 'But then I haven't got the sort of talents he has.'

Lomax threw his head back, his voice rising to a delighted squeal. 'Yeesss . . . I know what you mean! But we mustn't underestimate old Quilty.' As Ransom walked away he shouted after him: 'Don't forget, Charles – we'll keep a place for you here!'

Ransom hurried off down the drive, aware of Lomax apostrophizing to himself on the steps. Quilter and the cheetah were playing about in the far corner of the garden, leaping and swerving at each other.

As he passed one of the ornamental fountains, its drained concrete basin half-filled with sticks and refuse, Miranda Lomax stepped out from behind the balustrade. She hovered beside the pathway, her white hair falling uncombed around her grimy robe. She was streaked with ash and dust, and as she gazed into the dried-up pool she reminded Ransom of an imbecile Ophelia looking for her resting-stream.

Her rose-bud mouth chewed emptily as she watched him. 'Goodbye, doctor,' she said. 'You'll be back.'

With this, she turned and disappeared among the dusty hedges.

18

The Yantras

To the south, the scarred ribbon of the highway wound off across the land, the wrecked vehicles scattered along its verges like the battle debris of a motorized army. Abandoned cars and trucks had been driven off at random into the fields, their seats pulled out into the dust. To Ransom, looking down as he crossed the hump of the motor-bridge, the road appeared to have been under a heavy artillery bombardment. Loose kerbstones lay across the pedestrian walks, and there were gaps in the stone balustrade where cars had been pushed over the edge into the river below. The roadway was littered with glass and torn pieces of chromium trim.

Ransom free-wheeled the car down the slip road to the river. Rather than take the highway, he had decided to sail the houseboat along the river to the sea, and then around the coast to an isolated bay or island. By this means he hoped to avoid the chaos on the overland route and the hazards of fighting for a foothold among the sand-dunes. With luck, enough water would remain in the river to carry him to its mouth. On the seat behind him was a large outboard motor he had taken from a looted ship's chandlers' on the north bank. He estimated that the journey would take him little more than two or three days.

Ransom stopped on the slip road. Ten feet from the houseboat the burnt-out hulks of two cars lay on their backs in the mud. The smoke from the exploding fuel tanks had blackened the paintwork of the craft, but otherwise it was intact. Ransom lifted the outboard motor from the seat and began to haul it down the embankment to the landing-stage. The fine dust rose around him in clouds, and after a dozen steps, sinking to his knees through the brittle crust, he stopped to let it clear. The air was in fever, the angular sections of the concrete embankment below the bridge reflecting the sunlight like Hindu yantras telling of the movement of the time-stations. He pressed on a few steps, huge pieces of the crust sliding around him in the dust-falls.

Then he saw the houseboat more clearly.

Ten feet from the edge of the channel, the craft was stranded high and dry above the water, its pontoon set in a trough of baked mud. It leaned on its side near the burnt-out cars, covered with the ash blown down from the banks.

Ransom let the outboard motor subside into the dust, and ploughed his way down to the houseboat. The sloping bank was covered with old cans and dead birds and fish. A few yards to his left the body of a dog lay in the sunlight by the edge of the water.

Ransom climbed up on to the jetty and gazed down at the houseboat, stranded with all his hopes on the bleached shore. This miniature universe, a capsule containing whatever future lay before him, had expired with everything else on the floor of the drained river. He brushed the dust off his sleeves and trousers, looking out at the mud flats rising from the centre of the lake. At his feet the swollen body of the dog was blurred by the heat, and for a moment the whole landscape seemed to be covered with corpses. The dead fish rotated slowly from their hooks in the drying sheds, and a spasm of dizziness made Ransom retch emptily.

Above him, on the embankment, a car's starting motor whined. Ransom crouched down, watching the line of villas and the dust-filled aerial canopies. Nothing moved on the opposite bank. The river was motionless, the stranded craft propped against each other.

The car's engine resumed its plaintive noise, and masked the creaking of the gangway as Ransom made his way up the embankment. He crossed the empty garden next to Catherine Austen's villa, then followed the drive down to the road.

Catherine Austen sat over the wheel in the car, thumb on the starter button. She looked up as Ransom approached, her hand reaching to the pistol on the seat.

'Dr Ransom?' She dropped the pistol and concentrated on the starter. 'What are you doing here? This damn thing won't go.'

Ransom leaned on the windshield, recovering his breath, and watched her efforts to start the engine. In the back of the car were two large suitcases and a canvas hold-all. She seemed tired and distracted, streaks of dust in her red hair.

'Are you going to the coast?' Ransom held the window open before she could wind it up. 'You know that Quilter has one of the cheetahs?'

'What?' The news surprised her. 'What do you mean — Where is it?'

'At Lomax's house. You're a little late in the day.'

'I couldn't sleep. There was all that shooting.' She looked up at him. 'Doctor, I must get to the zoo. After last night the animals will be out of their minds.'

'If they're still there. By now Quilter and Whitman are probably running around with the entire menagerie. Catherine, it's time to leave.'

'I know, but . . .' She drummed at the wheel, glancing up at Ransom as if hopefully half-recognizing a forgotten friend, trying to find her compass in his drawn face with its ragged beard.

Leaving her, Ransom ran down the road to the next house. A car was parked in the open garage. He lifted the bonnet, and loosened the terminals of the battery. He slid the heavy unit out of its rack and carried it back to Catherine's car. After he had exchanged the batteries he gestured her along the seat. 'Let me try.'

She made room for him at the wheel. The fresh battery started the engine after a few turns. Without speaking, Ransom set off towards the motor-bridge. As they reached the junction he hesitated, wondering whether to accelerate southwards down the highway. Then he felt Catherine's hand on his arm. She was looking out over the bleached bed of the river, and at the brittle trees along the banks, ciphers suspended in the warm air. Ransom began to speak, but this cryptic alphabet seemed to overrule anything he might say.

He crossed the bridge and turned left into a side-road. Sooner or later he would have to leave Catherine. Her barely conscious determination to stay on reminded him of his own first hopes of isolating himself among the wastes of the new desert, putting an end to time and its erosions. But now a very different kind of time was being imposed upon them.

'Catherine, I know what you —'

Thirty yards ahead a driverless car rolled across the road. Ransom pressed hard on the brakes, pulling the car to a halt and throwing Catherine forward against the windshield.

He rolled her back on to the seat and searched for the wound on her forehead. A swarm of dark-suited men filled the street around them. Ransom picked up the revolver, and then saw the hard plump face of the bo'sun Saul peering at him through the window.

'Get them out! Clear the road!' A dozen hands seized the bonnet and jerked it into the air. A knife flashed in the bo'sun's brightly scarred hand and cut through the top hose of the radiator. Behind him the tall figure of Jonas hove into view, long arms raised as if feeling his way through darkness.

Ransom restarted the engine and slipped the gear lever into reverse. Flooring the accelerator, he flung the car backwards. The bonnet slammed down on the fingers tearing at the engine leads, sending up bellows of pain.

Steering over his shoulder, Ransom reversed along the street, hitting the parked vehicles as he swerved from left to right. Catherine leaned against the door, nursing her bruised head with one hand.

Ransom misjudged the corner, and the car jolted to a halt against the side of a truck. Steadying Catherine with one hand, he watched the gang setting off after them. Jonas stood on the roof of a car, one arm pointing towards them.

Ransom opened his door and pulled Catherine out into the road. She pushed her hair back with a feeble hand.

'Come on!' Taking her hand, he set off along a gravel-covered lane that ran down to the embankment. Helped by the sloping ground, they reached the slip road. Ransom pointed up to the motor-bridge. Two men moved along the balustrade. 'We'll have to wade across the river.'

As the dust clouds rose into the air behind them there was a shout from the bridge.

Catherine took Ransom's arm. 'Over there! Who's that boy?'

'Philip!' Ransom waved with both hands. Philip Jordan was standing near the houseboat on the other side of the river, looking down at the outboard motor Ransom had abandoned. His skiff, secured by the pole, was propped against the shore. With a quick glance at the men signalling from the motor-bridge, he side-stepped down the bank.

Freeing his pole, he jumped aboard. The craft's momentum carried it across the channel.

'Doctor! I thought you'd gone!'

He helped Ransom and Catherine Austen into the craft and pushed off. A shot rang out in warning. Four or five men, led by Jonas, crossed the slip road, and made their way down the embankment. The bo'sun brought up the rear, a long-barrelled rifle in his hands.

Jonas's stiff figure strode down the slope, black boots sending up clouds of dust. His men stumbled behind him, Saul cursing as he slipped and fell on his hands, but Jonas pressed on ahead of them.

The skiff stopped short of the bank as Philip Jordan scanned the river and approaches, uncertain which direction to take. Ransom leaned from the prow across the short interval of water. Blowing the dust from the breech of the rifle, the bo'sun levelled it at them. A bullet sang over their heads like a demented insect. 'Philip, forget the boat! We've got to leave now!'

Philip crouched behind his pole as Saul reloaded the rifle. 'Doctor, I can't . . . Quilter is —'

'Damn Quilter!' Ransom waved the pistol at Catherine, who was on her knees, holding tightly to the sides of the craft. 'Paddle with your hands! Philip, listen to me—!'

Jonas and his men had reached the water's edge, little more than a few boat-lengths away. Saul levelled the rifle at Philip, but Jonas stepped forward and knocked the weapon from his hands. His dark eyes gazed at the occupants of the skiff. He stepped on to a spur of rock, and for fully half a minute, oblivious of the pistol in Ransom's hand, stared down at the boat.

'Philip!' he shouted. 'Boy, come here!'

As his name echoed away across the drained river Philip Jordan turned, his hands clenching the pole for support. He looked up at the hawk-faced man glaring down at him.

'Philip . . . come!' Jonas's voice tolled like a harsh bell over the oily water.

Philip Jordan shook his head, hands grasping at the pole. Above him, like a hostile jury, a line of faces looked down from the bridge. Philip seized the pole and lifted it horizontally from the water, as if to bar the way to Jonas.

'Doctor . . . ?' he called over his shoulder.

'The bank, Philip!'

'No!' With a cry, looking back for the last time at the dark figure of Jonas, Philip leaned on the pole and punted the boat upstream towards the drained lake. The men on the bank surged forward around the bo'sun, shouting for the rifle, but the skiff darted behind the bulk of a lighter, then swung away again, its prow lifting like an arrow. Philip whipped the pole in and out, the water racing between his hands off the wet shaft.

'I'll go with you, doctor. But first . . .' He released the pole, then crouched down as the skiff surged across a patch of open water. 'First I must bring my father.'

Ransom reached forward to take Catherine's hand. He watched the youth as he manoeuvred them swiftly around the bend towards the lake, seeing in his face the arrow-like features of the black-garbed man standing on the shore while his men fought around him in the dust.

19

Mr Jordan

For an hour they followed the residue of the river as it wound across the lake. The channel narrowed, sometimes to little more than fifteen feet in width, at others dividing into thin streams that disappeared among the dunes and mudbanks. Stranded yachts lay on the slopes, streaked with the scum-lines of the receding water. The bed of the lake, almost drained, was now an inland beach of white dunes covered with pieces of blanched timber and driftwood. Along the bank the dried marsh-grass formed a burnt palisade.

They left the main channel and followed one of the small tributaries. They passed the remains of an old shack. Beside it a pier jutted out above the remains of grass that had seeded itself the previous summer when the water level had already fallen several feet. Working his pole tirelessly, Philip turned the craft like a key through the nexus of creeks, his face hidden behind his shoulder as he avoided Ransom's gaze. Once they stopped and he ordered them out, then ported the craft across a narrow saddle to the next stream. They passed the cylinder of a rusting distillation unit built out on the bed, its leaning towers like the barrels of some eccentric artillery in mutiny against the sky. Everywhere the bodies of voles and waterfowl lay among the weeds.

At length the stream flowed through a series of scrub-covered dunes, and they emerged into a small drained lagoon. In the centre, touched briefly by the stream as it disappeared beyond, was an ancient sailing barge, sitting squarely on the caked mud. All the craft they had passed had been stained and streaked with dirt, but the barge was immaculate, its hull shining in the sunlight in a brilliant patchwork of colours. The brass port-holes were freshly polished. A white landing-stage stood by the barge, a roped gangway leading to the deck. The mast, stripped of its rigging and fitted with a cross-tree, had been varnished to the brass annulus at its peak.

'Philip, what on earth——?' Ransom began. He felt Catherine's hand warningly on his arm. Philip beached the craft ten feet from the landing-stage and beckoned them aboard. He hesitated at the companion-head. 'I'll need your help, doctor,' he said, in an uncertain voice that reminded Ransom of his gruff waif's croak. He pointed to the cabin and deckwork, and added with a note of pride: 'It's an old wreck, you understand. Put together from any scraps I could find.'

He led the way down into the dark cabin. Sitting upright in a rocking chair in the centre of the spartan chamber was a grey-haired negro. He wore a faded khaki shirt and corduroy trousers, darned with a patchwork of laborious stitching. At first Ransom assumed from his broad shoulders and domed head that he was in late middle age, but as the light cleared he saw from his stick-like shoulders and legs that he was at least seventy-five years old. Despite his advanced age he held himself erect, his lined patrician head turning as Philip came towards him. The faint light through the shuttered port-holes was reflected in his opaque, blind eyes.

Philip bent down beside him. 'Father, it's time for us to leave. We must go south to the coast.'

The old negro nodded. 'I understand, Philip. Perhaps you would introduce me to your friends?'

'They will come with us to help. This is Dr Ransom and Miss —'

'Austen. Catherine Austen.' She stepped forward and touched the negro's claw-like hand. 'It's a pleasure, Mr Jordan.'

Ransom glanced around the cabin. Obviously there was no blood-link between Philip and the elderly negro, but he assumed that this blind old man was the youth's foster-father, the invisible presence he had felt behind Philip for so many years. A thousand puzzles were solved – this was why Philip always took his food away to eat, and why, despite Ransom's generous gifts during the winter, he was often close to starvation.

'Philip has told me of you a great deal, doctor,' the old man said in his soft voice. 'I have always known you to be a good friend to him.'

Ransom took the old man's hand, which held his own with a kind of gentle nervousness, its fingertips moving quickly as if reading a huge Braille character.

'That's why I want us to leave now, Mr Jordan,' Ransom said, 'before the drought begins to break up the land. Are you well enough to travel?'

The hint of an implied negative made Philip Jordan bridle. 'Of course he is!' He stepped between Ransom and the old man. 'Don't worry, Father, I won't leave you.'

'Thank you, Philip.' The old man's voice was still soft. 'Perhaps you would get ready. Take only what water and food you can carry conveniently.' As Philip moved away to the galley the old negro said: 'Dr Ransom, may I speak with you?'

When they were alone, he raised his sightless eyes towards Ransom. 'It will be a long journey, doctor, perhaps longer for you than for me. You will understand me when I say it will really begin when we get to the beach.'

'I agree,' Ransom said. 'It should be clear until we reach the coast.'

'Of course.' The negro smiled, his great domed head veined like a teak globe of the earth. 'I shall be a great burden to you, doctor, I would rather stay here than be left by the roadside later. May I ask you to be honest with yourself?'

Ransom stood up. Over his shoulder he could see Catherine Austen resting on the tiller in the sunlight, her hair lifting in the air like the fleece of some Homeric ram. The negro's question irritated him. Partly he resented the old man for having taken advantage of him for so many years, but even more for his assumption that Ransom could still make a simple choice between helping him on the one hand and abandoning him on the other. After the events of the previous days, he already felt that in the new landscape around them humanitarian considerations were becoming irrelevant.

'Doctor?'

'Mr Jordan, I daren't be honest with myself. Most known motives are so suspect these days that I doubt whether the hidden ones are any better. All the same, I'll try to get you to the beach.'

20

The Burning City

Shortly before dusk they began their return journey down the river. Ransom and Philip Jordan stood at bow and stern, each working a punt-pole, while Catherine and the old man sat amidships under a makeshift awning.

Around them the baked white surface of the lake stretched from horizon to horizon. Half a mile from the town, where they joined the main channel, a siren sounded into the hot afternoon air. Philip Jordan pointed two hundred yards to starboard, where Captain Tulloch's river steamer sat in a land-locked pool of water. Pennants flying and deck canvas trim over the rows of polished seats, the steamer's engines worked at full ahead, its high prow nudging the curve of a huge sand-flat. The screws turned tirelessly, churning the black water into a thick foam. Deserted by his helmsman, Captain Tulloch stood behind the wheel, sounding his siren at the dead flank of the dune as he nudged away at it, as if trying to wake a sleeping whale.

'Doctor . . . ?' Philip called out, but Ransom shook his head. They swept past, the sounds of the siren receding behind them in the haze.

They reached Hamilton at dusk, and rested behind the rusting hull of a dredger moored among the mud-floats at the entrance to the lake. In the fading light the old negro slept peacefully, sitting upright in the boat with his head against the metal posts of the awning. Beside him Catherine Austen leaned her elbows on the two jerrycans of water Philip had saved, head forward on her wrists.

As darkness settled over the river Ransom went up on to the bridge of the dredger, where Philip Jordan pointed towards the distant city. Huge fires were burning along the skyline; the flames swept off the roof-tops as the canopies of smoke lifted into the air over their heads.

'They're burning Mount Royal,' Ransom said. 'Lomax and Quilter.' As the light flickered in Philip Jordan's face Ransom saw again the beaked profile of Jonas. He turned back to the fires and began to count them.

An hour later they left the skiff and walked forward down the drained bed. The heat of the waterfront fires drove across the river like a burning sirocco. The entire horizon was ablaze, enormous fires raging on the outskirts of the city. Hamilton burned along the northern bank of the river, the flames sweeping down the streets. The boat-houses by the quays were on fire, the hundreds of fish illuminated in the dancing light. Overhead, myriads of glowing cinders sailed past like fireflies, and lay in the fields to the south as if the soil itself was beginning to burn.

'The lions!' Catherine shouted. 'Doctor, I can hear them!' She ran forward to the edge of the water, her face lit by the flames.

'Miss Austen!' Philip Jordan took her arm. Above the embankment of the motor-bridge, illuminated like an immense screen, stood one of the maned lions. It climbed on to the balustrade and looked down at the inferno below, then leapt away into the darkness. They heard a shout from the slip road, and one of the fishermen raced past the burning quays, the lion hunting him through the shadows.

They climbed up the bank to the shelter of the houses on the south shore of the river. A figure moved behind one of the stranded launches. A crone swathed in a bundle of rags clutched at Ransom before he could push her away.

'Doctor, you wouldn't be leaving an old body like Ma Quilter? To the taggers and the terrible flames, for pity's sake?'

'Mrs Quilter!' Ransom steadied her, half-afraid that the fumes of whisky that enveloped her might ignite them both. 'What are you doing here?'

'Looking for my boy, doctor . . .' She gestured like a distraught witch at the opposite bank, her face beaked and fearful in the pulsing light. 'It's that Lomax and his filthy Miranda, they've stolen my boy!'

Ransom propelled her up the slope. Catherine and Philip, the old negro carried between them, had scaled the bank and were crouching behind the wall in one of the gardens. The falling cinders flickered around them. As if set off by some pre-arranged signal, the whole of the lakeside town was burning simultaneously. Only Lomax's house, at the eye of this hurricane, was immune. Searching for his own home among the collapsing roofs, Ransom heard more shouts carried above the roaring timbers, and saw the two cheetahs racing in pursuit down the burning corridors.

'Philip!'

The cry came to them in a familiar demented voice across the river. Mrs Quilter turned, peering blindly into the flames, and shouted hoarsely: 'That's my boy! That's my old Quilty come for his Ma!'

'Philip . . . !' The running figure of Quilter approached the bank through the streets across the river, an unwieldy flapping object in his arms. He reached the open shore, shouting Jordan's name again, and then lifted his arms and released the bird. The black swan, still stained by the oil, lifted vigorously, its long neck stretched like the shaft of a spear towards Philip Jordan. Quilter watched as it crossed the river, wings working powerfully, the burning cinders falling around it. As it flew over, disappearing in a wide arc on the glowing tide of air, Philip waved to Quilter, who stood gazing after them as they faded from sight, his pensive face flickering in the firelight like a lost child's.

21

Journey to the Sea

By dawn the next morning they had covered some five miles to the south. All night the city had burned behind them, and Ransom pushed the small party along as fast as he could, fearing that Jonas and the fishermen had been driven across the motor-bridge. But the road behind them remained empty, receding into the flaring darkness.

At intervals they rested, sitting in the back seats of the cars abandoned along the roadway. As the fires of the city flickered in the driving mirrors, Ransom and the others slept intermittently, but Mrs Quilter spent the night scurrying from one car to another, sitting in the darkness and manipulating the controls. Once she pressed a horn, and the dull blare sounded away down the empty road.

Her new-found passion for automobiles was unabated the following morning. As Ransom and Philip Jordan limped along through the warm dawn light, the old negro borne between them in his litter, she accidentally started one of the cars.

'What would my Quilty think of me now, doctor?' she asked when Ransom reached her. He tried to protect the gear lever from her rapacious hands as the engine roared and raced under her dancing feet.

Five minutes later, when Ransom at last persuaded her to move along the seat, they set off in the car. To Ransom's surprise the engine was in perfect order, the fuel tank half full. Looking out at the vehicles abandoned along the road, Ransom assumed that they had been left there during the tremendous traffic jams the previous week. Stalled in motionless glaciers of metal that reached over the plains as far as the horizon, their occupants must have given up in despair and decided to walk the remaining miles.

Behind them the city disappeared from sight, but twenty-five miles farther to the south Ransom could still see the smoke staining the sky. On either side of them, beyond the vehicles driven on to the verges, the fields stretched away into the morning haze, their surfaces like buckled plates of rust. Isolated farmhouses, the dust drifting against their boarded windows, stood at the end of rutted lanes. Everywhere the bright bones of dead cattle lay by the empty water troughs.

For three hours they drove on, twice stopping to exchange cars when the tyres were punctured by the glass and metal on the road. They passed through a succession of deserted farm towns, then sped towards the coastal hills hidden below the horizon.

None of them spoke during this time. Mrs Quilter and Catherine sat in the back, staring out at the empty vehicles along the road. Between them, insulated by his blindness from the transformation of the landscape, the old negro sat with his head erect, stoically accepting the jolts and swerves of the car. Now and then he would murmur to Philip as the latter leaned back to steady his foster-father. Already Ransom sensed that his own bonds with Philip, formed within the margins of the river, had come to an end with the river's death and their departure.

The gradient began to descend as they entered the approaches to the river crossing. The numbers of abandoned cars increased. Ransom drove slowly along the one lane still open. The steel spans of the bridge rose above the stalled cars and trucks, which were carried over the hump like scrap metal on a conveyor.

A quarter of a mile from the bridge they were forced to stop, wedged between the converging traffic lanes. Ransom walked ahead and climbed on to the parapet. Originally some four hundred yards wide at this point, the river was almost drained. The thin creek wound its way like a tired serpent along the bleached white bed. Rusting lighters lay along the banks, which jutted into the air like lost cliffs facing each other across a desert. Despite the bridge and the embankment on the opposite shore, the existence of the river was now only notional, the drained bed merging into the surface of the land.

Looking up at the bridge, Ransom realized what had caused the traffic jam at its approaches. The central span, a section some one hundred feet long, had been blown up by a demolition team, and the steel cantilevers rested stiffly on the river bed, the edges of the roadway torn like metal pith. In the entrance to the bridge three army trucks had been shackled together as block vehicles. Their bonnets and driving cabins had been crushed into each other.

'Why blow up the bridge?' Philip Jordan asked as they made their way down on to the river bed. 'Don't they want people to reach the coast?'

'Perhaps not, Philip.' Ransom held to the poles of the litter as he found his footing in the crust. 'There's only so much beach.'

Several cars had been driven down off the embankment in an attempt to cross the river. They lay half-buried in the drifts of dust, slopes of fine powder covering their seats and dashboards. Mrs Quilter lingered by them, as if hoping that they might suddenly spring to life again, then gathered her silks around her and shuffled off on Catherine Austen's arm.

They reached the flat bed of the main channel and

walked past the collapsed mid-section of the bridge. The detonation leads looped back to the south shore. Listening for any sounds of traffic ahead, Ransom tripped, nearly dropping Mr Jordan.

'Dr Ransom, please rest for a moment,' the old negro apologized. 'I am sorry to be this burden to you.'

'Not at all. I was thinking of something else.' Ransom lowered the poles and wiped his face. During their journey to the south he had felt an increasing sense of vacuum, as if he was pointlessly following a vestigial instinct that no longer had any real meaning for him. The four people with him were becoming more and more shadowy, residues of themselves as notional as the empty river. He watched Catherine and Mrs Quilter climb on to a fallen steel girder that spanned the stream, already seeing them only in terms of the sand and dust, the eroding slopes and concealed shadows.

'Doctor.' Philip touched his arm. 'Over there.'

He followed Philip's raised hand. Two hundred yards away the solitary figure of a man was walking along the drained white channel. He was moving upstream away from them, a few feet from the narrow creek of black water at which, now and then, he cast a vague eye, as if out on a quiet reflective stroll. He wore a suit of faded cotton, almost the colour of the bleached deck around him, but carried no equipment, apparently unaware of the sunlight on his head and shoulders.

'Where's he going?' Philip asked. 'Shall I stop him?'

'No, leave him.' Without thinking, Ransom walked forward a few paces, as if following the man. He waited, almost expecting to see a dog appear and run around the man's heels. The absolute isolation of the chalk-white promenade, with its empty perspectives, focused an intense light upon the solitary traveller. For some reason, his strange figure, detached from the pressing anxieties of the drought and exodus, seemed a compass of all the unstated motives that Ransom had been forced to repress during the previous days.

'Doctor, it's time to go on.'

'Just a moment, Philip.'

The significance of this figure, disappearing along the heat-glazed bed, still eluded Ransom as he sat with the others on the south embankment. Philip lit a small fire and prepared a meal of boiled rice. Ransom swallowed a few spoonfuls of the tasteless gruel, and then gave his plate to Mr Jordan. Even Catherine Austen, leaning one arm on his shoulder as he gazed out over the broad bed of the river, failed to distract him. With an effort he joined the others as they climbed the embankment, pulling Mr Jordan behind them.

The road to the south was clear of cars. The remains of an army post were scattered along the verge. Cooking utensils hung from tripods outside the deserted tents, and a truck lay on its side among the bales of wire and old tyres.

Mrs Quilter snorted in disgust. 'Where's all the cars gone to, doctor? We'll be wanting one for my old legs, you know.'

'There may be some soon. You'll simply have to walk until we find one.'

Already Ransom was losing interest in her. The poles of the litter pressed into his shoulders. He laboured along the road, thinking of the solitary man on the river bed.

22

Multiplication of the Arcs

Two hours later, after they had found a car, they reached the foothills of the coastal range. They followed the road upwards, winding past burnt-out orchards and groves of brittle trees like the remnants of a petrified forest. Around them in the hills drifted the smoke of small fires, the white plumes wandering down the valleys. Here and there they saw the low roofs of primitive hovels built on the crests. The wooded slopes below were littered with the shells of cars tipped over the road. They began to descend through a narrow cutting, and emerged on to one side of a wide canyon. At the bottom, in the bed of a dried-up stream, a timber fire burned briskly. Two men worked beside a small still, their bare chests blackened by charcoal, ignoring the passing car.

The trees receded to give them a view of a distant headland partly veiled by the long plumes of smoke moving inland. Suddenly the car was filled with the sharp tang of brine. A final bend lay ahead, and in front of them was the grey hazy disc of the sea. On the edge of the bluff, partly blocking their view, two men sat on the roof of a car, gazing down at the coastal shelf below. They glanced at the approaching car, their faces thin and drawn in the sunlight. More cars were parked around the bend, and along the road as it wound downwards to the shore. People sat on the roofs and bonnets, staring out at the sea.

Ransom stopped the car and switched off the engine. Below them, stretching along the entire extent of the coastal shelf, were tens of thousands of cars and trailers, jammed together like vehicles in an immense parking lot. Tents and wooden shacks were squeezed between them, packed more and more tightly as they neared the beach, where they overran the dunes and sand-flats. A small group of naval craft – grey-hulled patrol boats and coastguard cutters – were moored a quarter of a mile off shore. Long metal piers had been built out into the water towards them, and there was no clear dividing line between the sea and the shore. At intervals along the dunes stood a number of large metal huts, almost the size of aircraft hangars. Around them tall distillation columns streamed into the air, their vapour mingling with the smoke of the fires burning across the whole eight-hundred-yard width of the coastal shelf. The distant sounds of machinery were carried across to the cliff, and for a moment the clanking noise of the pumping gear and the bright galvanized iron roofs along the dunes made the whole area resemble a gigantic beach-side fun fair, the car-parks crammed with millions of would-be participants.

Catherine Austen took Ransom's arm. 'Charles, we'll never get down there.'

Ransom opened his door. He had expected the beach to be crowded, but not the vast concourse below, a meaningless replication of identity in which an infinite number of doubles of himself were being generated by a cancerous division of time. He peered down through the smoke, trying to find even a single free space. Here and there, in the garden of a house or behind a derelict filling station, there was room for a few more vehicles, but the approach lanes were closed. One or two cars crawled about the churned-up roadways, like ants blindly moving with no notion of their overall direction, but otherwise the whole shore had settled into an immovable jam. Everywhere people sat on the roofs of cars and trailers, staring out through the smoke towards the sea.

The only signs of organized activity came from the beach area. Trucks sped along a road between the dunes, and the lines of cars parked behind the metal huts formed neat patterns. Lines of tents shone in the sunlight, grouped around communal kitchens and service units.

'Wait here.' Ransom stepped from the car and walked along to the two men sitting on the roof of the car near by.

He nodded to them. 'We've just arrived. How do we get down to the beach?'

The older of the two, a man of sixty, ignored Ransom. He was staring, not at the congestion below, but at the far horizon, where the sea dissolved in a pale haze. The fixity of his expression reminded Ransom of the obsessed cloud-watchers on their towers in Hamilton.

'We need water,' Ransom explained. 'We've come a hundred miles today. There's an elderly cripple in the car.'

The other man, a trilby pulled down to shade his face, glanced down at Ransom. He seemed to detect the lack of conviction in Ransom's voice, and gave him a thin smile, almost of encouragement, as if Ransom had successfully passed this first hurdle.

Ransom walked back to the car. The road wound down the side of the cliff, past the people who had retreated to this last vantage point. It levelled out and approached the nearest of the shanty camps.

Immediately all sense of the sea was lost, the distant dunes hidden by the roofs of trucks and trailers, and by the drifting smoke of garbage fires. Thousands of people squatted among the cars or sat on their doorsteps. Small groups of men moved about silently. The road divided, one section running parallel with the beach along the foot of the hills, the other heading diagonally towards the sea. Ransom stopped at the junction and searched for any signs of police or an army control post. On their right, smashed to pieces at the roadside, were the remains of a large sign, the metal scaffolding stripped of its wooden panels.

Choosing the beachward road, Ransom entered the shanty town. Twenty yards ahead was a crude barricade. As they stopped, four or five men appeared from the doorways of the trailers. They waved at Ransom, gesturing him back. One of them carried a metal fencing post. He walked up to the car and banged it against the grille.

Ransom held his ground. Ahead the road disappeared within fifty yards into the jungle of shacks and cars. The ground was churned into huge ruts.

A dirty hand spread across the windshield. A man's unshaven face poked through the window like a muzzle. 'Come on, mister! Back the hell out of here!'

Ransom started to argue, but then gave up and reversed back to the road junction. They set off along the coast road below the cliffs. The motor camps stretched ahead of them to the right, the backs of trailers jutting out over the empty pavement. On the left, where the cliffs had been cut back at intervals to provide small lay-bys, single families squatted under makeshift awnings, out of sight of sea and sky, gazing at the camps separating them from the beach.

Half a mile ahead they climbed a small rise, and could see the endless extent of the camps, reaching far into the haze beyond the cape ten miles away. Ransom stopped at a deserted filling station, and peered down a narrow lane that ran into the trailer camp. Small children squatted with their mothers, watching the menfolk stand and argue. The smoke of garbage fires drifted across the blank sky, and the air was touched by the sweet smells of unburied sewage.

A few dust-streaked cars cruised past in the opposite

direction, faces pressed to the windows as their occupants searched for some foothold off the road.

Ransom pointed to the licence plates. 'Some of these people must have been driving along the coast for days.' He opened the door. 'There's no point in going on any farther. I'll get out and have another look around.'

Leaving Philip Jordan to guard the car, Ransom walked down the road, glancing between the lines of vehicles. People were lying about in the shade, or had walled in the narrow alleys with squares of canvas. Farther in, a crowd of people had surrounded a large chromium-sided trailer and were rocking it from side to side, drumming on the doors and windows with spades and pick-axe handles.

An old cigarette kiosk leaned against a concrete telegraph pole by the side of the road. Ransom managed to lift one foot on to the counter, and pulled himself up on to the roof. Far into the distance the silver flanks of the metal hangars along the shore glistened in the sunlight like an unattainable El Dorado. The sounds of pumping equipment drummed across to him, overlaid by the murmur and babble of the people in the camps.

Below Ransom, in a small niche off the edge of the pavement, a middle-aged man in shirt sleeves was working a primus stove below the awning of his trailer. This miniature vehicle was little larger than a sedan chair. Sitting inside the doorway was his wife, a sedate round-faced woman in a floral dress. The primus flared in the heat, warming a metal teapot.

Ransom climbed down and approached the man. He had the intelligent, sensitive eyes of a watch-maker. As Ransom came up he poured the tea into two cups on a tray.

'Herbert,' his wife called.

'It's all right, dear.'

Ransom bent down beside him, nodding to the woman. 'Do you mind if I talk to you?'

'Go ahead,' the man said. 'But I've no water to spare.'

'That's all right. I've just arrived with some friends,' Ransom said. 'We intended to reach the beach, but it looks as if we're too late.'

The man nodded, stirring the tea. 'You probably are,' he agreed. 'Still, I wouldn't worry, we're not much better off.' He added: 'We've been here two days.'

'We were on the road three,' his wife interjected. 'Tell him about that, Herbert.'

'He's been on the road too, dear.'

'What chance is there of getting on to the shore?' Ransom asked. 'We're going to need some water soon. Aren't there any police around?'

The man finished sipping his tea. 'Let me explain. Perhaps you couldn't see from up there, but all along the beach there's a double wire fence. The army and police are on the other side. Every day they let a few people through. Behind those sheds there are big distillation units. They say there'll be plenty of water soon and everyone should stay where they are.' He smiled faintly. 'Boiling and condensing water is a long job, you need cooling towers a hundred feet high.'

'What happens if you climb through the wire on to the beach?'

'*If* you climb through. The army are all right, but last night the militia units were shooting at the people trying to cross between the fences. Machine-gunned them down in the spotlights.'

Ransom noticed Philip Jordan and Catherine standing on the pavement by the kiosk. From their faces he could see that they were frightened he might leave them when they were still a few hundred yards short of the beach.

'But what about the government evacuation plans?' Ransom asked. 'Those beach cards and so on . . .' He stood up when the other made no reply. 'What do you plan to do?'

The man gazed at Ransom with his calm eyes. 'Sit here and wait.' He gestured around at the camp. 'This won't last for ever. Already most of these people have only a day's water left. Sooner or later they'll break out. My guess is that by the time they reach the water they'll be thinned out enough for Ethel and me to have all we want.'

His wife nodded in agreement, sipping her tea.

23

The Fairground

They set off along the road again. The hills began to recede, the road turning until it moved almost directly inland. They had reached the margins of the river estuary. The funnel-shaped area had once been bordered by marshes and sand-flats, and the low-lying ground still seemed damp and gloomy, despite the hot sunlight breaking across the dry grass. The hundreds of vehicles parked among the dunes and hillocks had sunk up to their axles in the soft sand, their roofs tilting in all directions. Ransom stopped by the edge of the road, the presence of the river-bed offering him a fleeting security. Three hundred yards away were the stout fencing posts of the perimeter wire, the barbed coils staked to the ground between them. A narrow strip of dunes and drained creeks separated this line from the inner fence. A quarter of a mile beyond the fence they could see a small section of the shore, the waves foaming on the washed sand. On either side of the empty channel dozens of huts were being erected, and bare-chested men worked quickly in the sunlight. Their energy, and the close proximity of the water behind their backs, contrasted painfully with the thousands of listless people watching from the dunes on the other side of the barbed wire.

Ransom stepped from the car. 'We'll try here. We're farther from the shore but there are fewer people. Perhaps they dislike the river for some reason.'

'What about the car?' Philip asked. He watched Ransom warily, as if reluctant to give up even the small security of the vehicle.

'Leave it. These people have brought everything with them, they're not going to abandon their cars when they're parked on the sand.' Ransom waited for the others to climb out but they sat inertly. 'Come on, Catherine. Mrs Quilter, you can sleep on the dunes tonight.'

'I don't know for sure, doctor.' Screwing up her face, she stepped from the car.

'What about you, Mr Jordan?' Ransom asked.

'Of course, doctor.' The negro still sat upright. 'Just settle me on the sand.'

'We're not on the sand.' Controlling his impatience, Ransom said: 'Philip, perhaps Mr Jordan could wait in the car. When we've set up some sort of post by the wire we'll come back and get him.'

'No, doctor.' Philip shook his head. 'If we can't take him in the litter I'll carry him myself.' Before Ransom could remonstrate he bent down and lifted the elderly negro from the car. His strong arms carried him like a child.

Ransom led the way, followed by Catherine and Mrs Quilter. The old woman fussed along, muttering at the people sitting in the hollows by their cars and trailers. Philip Jordan was fifty yards behind them, watching his footing in the churned sand, the old negro in his arms. Soon the road was lost to sight, and the stench of the encampment filled their lungs. A maze of pathways turned between the vehicles and among the dry, grass-topped dunes. Seeing the jerrycan partly hidden inside his jacket, children wheeled at Ransom with empty cups. Small groups of men, unshaven and stained with dust, argued hotly with each other, pointing towards the fence. The nearer to this obstacle the higher tempers seemed to flare, as if the earlier arrivals — many of whom, to judge by their camping equipment, had been there for a week or more — realized that the great concourse pressing behind them made it less and less likely that they themselves would ever reach the sea.

Fortunately the extension of the perimeter fence into the mouth of the river allowed Ransom to approach the wire without having to advance directly towards the sea. Once or twice he found his way barred by men with shot-guns in their hands, waving him away from a private encampment.

An hour later Ransom reached a point some twenty yards from the outer fence, in a narrow hollow between two groups of trailers. They were partly sheltered from the sunlight by the sticks of coarse grass on the crests of the surrounding hillocks. Catherine and Mrs Quilter sat down and rested, waiting for Philip Jordan to appear. The flies and mosquitoes buzzed around them, the stench from the once marshy ground thickening the air. The trailers near by belonged to two circus families, who had moved down to the coast with part of their travelling fun fair. The gilt-painted canopies of two merry-go-rounds rose above the dunes, the antique horses on their spiral pinions lend-ing a carnival air to the scene. The dark-eyed womenfolk and their daughters sat like a coven of witches around the ornamental traction engine in the centre, watching the distant shore as if expecting some monstrous fish to be cast up out of the water.

'What about Philip and Mr Jordan?' Catherine asked when they had not appeared. 'Shouldn't we go back and look for them?'

Lamely, Ransom said: 'They'll probably get here later. We can't risk leaving here, Catherine.'

Mrs Quilter sat back against the broken earth. Shaking the flies off her dusty silks, she muttered to herself as if unable to comprehend what they were doing in this fly-infested hollow.

Ransom climbed on to the crest of the dune. However depressing, the lack of loyalty towards Philip Jordan did not surprise him. With their return to the drained river he felt again the sense of isolation in time that he had known when he stood on the deck of his houseboat, looking out at the stranded objects on the dry bed around him. Here, where the estuary widened, the distances separating him from the others had become even greater. In time, the sand drifting across the dunes would reunite them on its own terms, but for the present each of them formed a self-contained and discreet world of his own.

Near by, a man in a straw hat lay among the dried grass, peering through the wire at the drained channel running towards the beach. A nexus of narrow creeks and small dunes separated them from the inner fence. Beyond this the recently erected huts were already filling. Several trucks stopped outside them, and some fifty or sixty people climbed out and hurried indoors with their suitcases.

A large truck came into view past the huts and headed towards the inner fence. It stopped there, and two soldiers jumped out and opened a wire gate. Rolling forward, the truck bumped across the dunes. As its engine raced noisily, Ransom noticed a concerted movement through the camp. People climbed down from the roofs of their trailers, others stepped from cars and pulled their children after them. Fifty yards away, where the truck stopped by the outer fence, the crowd gathered some three or four hundred strong. The soldiers lowered a fifty-gallon drum off the tail-board and rolled it across the ground.

There were a few shouts as the drum neared the fence, but neither of the soldiers looked up. As they pushed it through the wire the crowd surged forward, drawn as much to these two isolated figures as to their cargo of water. As they climbed into the truck again the crowd fell silent, then came to and burst into a chorus of jeers. The shouts followed the truck as it crossed the open interval and disappeared through the gate. With a whoop, the drum was lifted into the air and borne away, then flung to the ground twenty yards from the fence.

As the spray from the scattered water formed ragged rainbows in the air, Ransom climbed down from the dune and rejoined the others in the hollow. Mrs Quilter appeared from the direction of the fun fair, the straw-hatted man following her. He beckoned Ransom towards him.

'You talk to him, dearie,' Mrs Quilter croaked. 'I told them what a marvellous doctor you are.'

The straw-hatted man was more precise. He took Ransom aside. 'The old Romany says you have a gun. Is that right?'

Ransom nodded cautiously. 'Fair enough. Why?'

'Can you use the gun? She says you're a doctor.'

'I can use it,' Ransom said. 'When?'

'Soon.' The man glanced at Ransom's grimy linen suit and then walked away to the merry-go-round, swinging himself through the antique horses.

24

The Bitter Sea

Soon after midnight Ransom lay on the crest of the dune. Around him echoed the night-sounds of the camps, and the embers of hundreds of fires smoked in the darkness. A sullen murmur, punctuated by shouts and gunfire farther along the beach, drifted across the sand-hills. Below him Catherine and Mrs Quilter lay together in the hollow, their eyes closed, but no one else was asleep. The dunes around him were covered with hundreds of watching figures. Listening to the uncertain movements, Ransom realized that there was no concerted plan of action, but that some dim instinct was gathering force and would propel everyone simultaneously at the wire.

The lights beyond the fences had been dimmed, and the dark outlines of the huts shone in the light reflected from the waves as they spilled on to the beaches. Only the pumping gear drummed steadily.

Above him somewhere, a wire twanged. Peering into the darkness, Ransom saw a man disappear through the fence, crawling down one of the drained channels.

'Catherine!' Ransom kicked some sand on to Catherine's shoulder. She looked up at him and then woke Mrs Quilter. 'Get ready to move!'

On their left, across the channel of the river, more firing broke out. Most of the tracers flew high into the air, their arcs carrying them away across the estuary, but Ransom could see that at least two of the sentries, presumably members of the locally recruited militia, were firing straight into the trailer camp.

Floodlights blazed down from a dozen posts along both fences. Crouching down, his arms motionless among the grass, Ransom waited for them to go out. He looked up as there was a roar from the open interval beyond the fence.

Crossing the dunes and creeks, in full view of the platoon of soldiers on the dunes above the inner fence, were some forty or fifty men. Shouting to each other, they jumped in and out of the shallow creeks, one or two of them stopping to fire at the floodlights. Unscathed, they reached the wire, and everywhere people started to climb to their feet and run forward into the floodlights.

Ransom reached down and took Catherine's arm. 'Come on!' he shouted. They scaled the shallow slope up to the fence. A wide section of the wire coil had been removed, and they crawled through, then darted down into a narrow creek. Dozens of other people were moving along with them, some pulling small children, others carrying rifles in their hands.

They were halfway across when a light machine-gun began to fire loosely over their heads from an emplacement below the huts, its harsh ripple coming in short bursts of two or three seconds. Partly hidden by the rolling ground, everyone pressed on, climbing through a gap cut in the inner fence. Then, ten yards from Ransom, a man was shot dead and fell back into the grass. Another was hit in the leg, and lay shouting on the ground as people ran past him.

Ransom pulled Catherine down into an empty basin. Everywhere men and women were rushing past in all directions. Several of the floodlights had gone out, and in the flaring darkness he could see men with carbines retreating to the dunes beyond the huts. To their left the open channel of the river ran to the sea, the beach washed like a silver mirror.

The scattered shooting resumed, the soldiers firing over the heads of the hundreds of people moving straight towards the sea. Taking Catherine by the arm, Ransom pulled her towards the opening of the inner fence. Behind them, more bodies lay among the dunes, tumbled awkwardly in the coarse grass.

Following an empty creek, they moved away from the huts. As they crouched down to rest before their final dash to the sea, a man stood up in the burnt grass ten feet above them. With a raised pistol he began to fire across the dunes, shooting straight at the people driven back by the soldiers.

Looking up at him, Ransom recognized the stocky shoulders and pugnacious face.

'Grady!' he called. 'Hold off, man!'

As they stumbled from their hiding-place Grady turned and searched the darkness below him. He levelled his pistol at them. He seemed to recognize Ransom, but gestured at him with the weapon.

'Go back!' he shouted hoarsely. 'Keep off, we came here first!'

More people appeared, running head down along the dry bed of the creek. Grady stared at them, his little face for a moment like an insane sparrow's. Raising his pistol, he fired blindly at Ransom's shadow. As Catherine crouched down on her knees. Ransom drew the pistol from his belt. Grady darted forward, his eyes searching the darkness among the clumps of grass, his small figure illuminated in the floodlights. Ransom waited. Then, holding the butt of the revolver in both hands, he stood up and shot Grady through the chest.

Ransom was kneeling over the little man, his own weapon lost somewhere in the creek, when a platoon of soldiers appeared out of the darkness. Lying down, they began to fire over the heads of the people farther down the creek.

A bare-headed lieutenant crawled over to Ransom. He glanced down at the body. 'One of ours?' he asked breathlessly.

'Grady,' Ransom said. The lieutenant peered about, and then jumped to his feet and ordered his men back up the slope towards the huts. The firing had slackened as the main impetus of the advance spent itself, and many people were retreating back to the fences. Others had got through and were running down to the water between the huts, ignored by the soldiers farther along the beach, who let them go by.

The lieutenant pushed Catherine behind the edge of the old sea-wall. To Ransom he shouted: 'Take his gun and keep firing! Over their heads, but if they come at you bring one of them down!'

The soldiers moved off and Ransom joined Catherine behind the wall. The sea was only fifty yards away, the waves sluicing across the wet sand. Exhausted by the noise, Catherine leaned limply against the wall.

Two or three figures came racing across the flat channel. Ransom raised his pistol, but they ran straight towards him. Then the last of them appeared, Philip Jordan with the old negro in his arms. He saw Ransom standing in front of him, the pistol raised in his hand, but ran on, limping on his bare feet.

Ransom threw away the pistol. All along the beach small groups of people were lying in the shallows as the waves splashed across them, watched by the soldiers. Some, unable to drink the water, were already climbing back on to the sand. Running after the others, Ransom saw Philip Jordan on his knees by the water's edge, lowering the old man to the waves. Ransom felt the water sting his legs, and then fell headlong into the shallows, his suit soaked by the receding waves, vomiting into the bitter stream.

Part Two

25

Dune Limbo

Under the empty winter sky the salt-dunes ran on for miles. Seldom varying more than a few feet from trough to crest, they shone damply in the cold air, the pools of brine disturbed by the inshore wind. Sometimes, in a distant foretaste of the spring to come, their crests would be touched with white streaks as a few crystals evaporated out into the sunlight, but by the early afternoon these began to deliquesce, and the grey flanks of the dunes would run with a pale light.

To the east and west the dunes stretched along the coast to the horizon, occasionally giving way to a small lake of stagnant brine or a lost creek cut off from the rest of its channel. To the south, in the direction of the sea, the dunes gradually became more shallow, extending into long salt flats. At high tide they were covered by a few inches of clear water, the narrowing causeways of firmer salt reaching out into the sea.

Nowhere was there a defined margin between the shore and sea, and the endless shallows formed the only dividing zone, land and water submerged in this grey liquid limbo. At intervals the skeleton of a derelict conveyor emerged from the salt and seemed to point towards the sea, but then, after a few hundred yards, sank from sight again. Gradually the pools of water congregated into larger lakes, small creeks formed into continuous channels, but the water never seemed to move. Even after an hour's walk, knee-deep in the dissolving slush, the sea remained as distant as ever, always present and yet lost beyond the horizon, haunting the cold mists that drifted across the salt-dunes.

To the north, the dunes steadily consolidated themselves, the pools of water between them never more than a few inches deep. Eventually, where they overran the shore, they rose into a series of large white hillocks, like industrial tippings, which partly concealed the coastal hills. The foreshore itself, over the former beaches, was covered by the slopes of dry salt running down to the dunes. The spires of ruined distillation columns rose into the air, and the roofs of metal huts carried off their foundations floated like half-submerged wrecks. Farther out there were the shells of pumping gear and the conveyors that had once carried the waste salt back into the sea.

A quarter of a mile from the shore, the hulks of two or three ships were buried to their upper decks in the salt, their grey superstructures reflected in the brine-pools. Small shacks of waste metal sheltered against their sides and beneath the overhang of the sterns. Outside the lean-to doors smoke drifted from the chimneys of crude stills.

Beside each of these dwellings, sometimes protected by a palisade of stakes, was a small pond of brine. The banks had been laboriously beaten into a hard margin, but the water seeping everywhere continually dissolved them. Despite the to and fro movements of the inhabitants of the salt wastes, no traces of their footsteps marked the surface, blurred within a few minutes by the leaking water.

Only towards the sea, far across the dunes and creeks, was there any activity.

26

The Lagoon

Shortly after dawn, as the tide extended across the margins of the coastal flats, the narrow creeks and channels began to fill with water. The long salt-dunes darkened with the moisture seeping through them, and sheets of open water spread outwards among the channels, carrying with them a few fish and nautiloids. Reaching towards the firmer shore, the cold water infiltrated among the saddles and culverts like the advance front of an invading army, its approach almost unnoticed. A cold wind blew overhead and dissolved in the dawn mists, lifting a few uneager gulls across the banks.

Almost a mile from the shore, the tide began to spill through a large breach in one of the salt-bars. The water sluiced outwards into a lagoon some three hundred yards in diameter, inundating the shallow dunes in the centre. As it filled this artificial basin, it smoothed itself into a mirror of the cloudless sky.

The margins of the lagoon had been raised a few feet above the level of the surrounding salt flats, and the wet crystals formed a continuous bank almost half a mile in length. As the water poured into the breach it carried away the nearer sections of the mouth, and then, as the tide began to slacken, swilled away along the banks.

Overhead the gulls dived, picking at the hundreds of fish swimming below the surface. In the equilibrium, the water ceased to move, and for a moment the great lagoon, and the long arms of brine seeping away northwards through the grey light, were like immense sheets of polished ice.

At this moment, a shout crossed the air. A dozen men rose from behind the bank surrounding the lagoon and with long paddles of whalebone began to shovel the wet salt into the breach. Sliding up to their waists in the grey slush, they worked furiously as the crystals drained backwards towards the sea. Their arms and chests were strung with strips of rag and rubber. They drove each other on with sharp cries and shouts, their backs bent as they ladled the salt up into the breach, trying to contain the water in the lagoon before the tide turned.

Watching them from the edge of the bank was a tall, thin-faced man wearing a sealskin cape over his left shoulder, his right hand on the shaft of his double-bladed paddle. His dark face, from which all flesh had been drained away, seemed to consist of a series of flint-like points, the sharp cheekbones and jaw almost piercing the hard skin. He gazed across the captured water, his eyes counting the fish that gleamed and darted. Over his shoulder he watched the tide recede, dissolving the banks as it moved along them. The men in the breach began to shout to him as the wet salt poured across them, sliding and falling as they struggled to hold back the bank. The man in the cape ignored them, jerking the sealskin with his shoulder, his eyes on the falling table of water beyond the banks and the shining deck of the trapped sea within the lagoon.

At the last moment, when the water seemed about to burst from the lagoon at a dozen points, he raised his paddle and swung it vigorously at the opposite bank. A cry like a gull's scream tore from his throat. As he raced off along the bank, leaving the exhausted men in the breach to drag themselves from the salt, a dozen men emerged from behind the northern bank. Their paddles whirling, they cut an opening in the wall twenty yards wide, then waded out to their chests in the water and drove it through the breach.

Carried by its own weight, the water poured in a torrent into the surrounding creeks, drawing the rest of the lagoon behind it. By the time the man in the cape had reached this new opening, half the lagoon had drained away, rushing out in a deep channel. Like a demented canal, it poured on towards the shore, washing away the smaller dunes in its path. It swerved to the north-east, the foam boiling around the bend, then entered a narrow channel cut between two dunes. Veering to the left, it set off again for the shore, the man in the cape racing along beside it. Now and then he stopped to scan the course ahead, where the artificial channel had been strengthened with banks of drier salt, then turned and shouted to his men. They followed along the banks, their paddles driving the water on as it raced past.

Abruptly, a section of the channel collapsed and water spilled away into the adjacent creeks. Shouting as he ran, the leader raced through the shallows, his two-bladed paddle hurling the water back. His men floundered after him, repairing the breach and driving the water up the slope.

Leaving them, the leader ran on ahead, where the others were paddling the main body of water across the damp dunes. Although still carried by its own momentum, the channel had widened into a gliding oval lake, the hundreds of fish tumbling about in the spinning currents. Every twenty yards, as the lake poured along, a dozen fish would be stranded behind, and two older men bringing up the rear tossed them back into the receding wake.

Guiding it with their blades, the men took up their

positions around the bows of the lake. At their prow, only a few feet from the front wave, the man in the cape piloted them across the varying contours. The lake coursed smoothly in and out of the channels, cruising over the shallow pools in its path. Half a mile from the shore it rilled along, still intact.

'Captain!' There was a shout from the two look-outs in the tail. 'Captain Jordan!'

Whirling in the damp salt, the leader raised his paddle and drove the oarsmen back along the shores of the lake. Two hundred yards away, a group of five or six men, heads lowered as they worked their short paddles, had broken down the bank on the western side of the lake and were driving the water outwards across the dunes.

Converging around both banks, the trappers raced towards them, their paddles flashing at the water. The pirates ignored them and worked away at the water, propelling it through the breach. Already a large pool some fifty yards wide had formed among the dunes. As the main body of the lake moved away, they ran down the bank and began to paddle the pool away across the shallows to the west.

Feet splashed after them through the brine, and the air was filled with whirling paddles and salt spray. Trying to recover the water they had lured with such effort from the sea, the trappers drove it back towards the lake. Some of them attacked the pirates, splintering the short paddles with their heavier blades. The dark-faced man in the seal-skin cape beat one man to his knees, snapping the bony shaft of his paddle with his foot, then clubbed another across the face, knocking him into the shallows. Warding off the flying blades, the pirates stumbled to their feet, pushing the water between their attackers' legs. Their leader, an older man with a red weal on his bearded face, shouted to them and they darted off in all directions, dividing the water into half a dozen pools which they drove away with their paddles and bare hands.

In the mêlée the main body of the lake had continued its gliding progress to the shore. The defenders broke off the attempt to recapture the water and ran after the lake, their rubber suits streaming with the cold salt. One or two of them stopped to shout over their shoulders, but the pirates had disappeared among the dunes. As the grey morning light gleamed in the wet slopes, their foot-falls were lost in the streaming salt.

27

The Tidal Waves

Nursing his cheek against the rubber pad on his shoulder, Ransom made his way among the watery dunes, steering the small pool through the hollows. Now and then, as the pool raced along under its own momentum, he stopped to peer over the surrounding crests, listening to the distant cries of Jordan and his men. Sooner or later a punitive expedition would be sent over to the beaches where the outcasts lived. At the prospect of smashed cabins and wrecked stills Ransom rallied himself and pressed on, guiding the pool through the dips. Little more than twenty feet wide, it contained half a dozen small fish. One of them was stranded at his feet and Ransom bent down and picked it up. Before he tossed it back into the water his frozen fingers felt its plump belly.

Three hundred yards to his right he caught a glimpse of Jonathan Grady propelling his pool towards his shack below a ruined salt-conveyor. Barely seventeen years old, he had been strong enough to take almost half the stolen water for himself, and drove it along untiringly through the winding channels.

The other four members of the band had disappeared among the salt flats. Ransom pushed himself ahead, the salty air stinging the weal on his face. By luck Jordan's paddle had caught him with the flat of its blade, or he would have been knocked unconscious and carried off to the summary justice of the Johnstone settlement. There his former friendship with the Reverend Johnstone, long-forgotten after ten years, would have been of little help. It was now necessary to go out a full mile from the shore to trap the sea – the salt abandoned during the previous years had begun to slide off the inner beach areas, raising the level of the offshore flats, and the theft of water had become the greatest crime for the communities along the coast.

Ransom shivered in the cold light, and tried to squeeze the moisture from the damp rags beneath his suit of rubber strips. Sewn together with pieces of fish-gut, the covering leaked at a dozen places. He and the other members of the band had set out three hours before dawn, following Jordan and his team over the grey dunes. They hid themselves in the darkness by the empty channel, waiting for the tide to turn, knowing they had only a few minutes to steal a small section of the lake. But for the need to steer the main body of water to the reservoir at the settlement, Jordan and his men would have caught them. One night soon, no doubt, they would deliberately sacrifice their catch to rid themselves for ever of Ransom and his band.

Ransom moved along beside the pool, steering it towards the distant tower of the wrecked lightship whose stern jutted from the sand a quarter of a mile away. Automatically he counted and recounted the fish swimming in front of him, wondering how long he could continue to prey on Jordan and his men. By now the sea was so far away, the shore so choked with salt, that only the larger and more skilful teams could trap the water and carry it back to the reservoirs. Three years earlier Ransom and the young Grady had been able to cut permanent channels through the salt, and at high tide enough water flowed down them to carry small catches of fish and crabs. Now, as the whole area had softened, the wet sliding salt made it impossible to keep any channel open for more than twenty yards, unless a huge team of men was used, digging the channel afresh as they moved ahead of the stream.

The remains of one of the metal conveyors jutted from the dunes ahead. Small pools of water gathered around the rusting legs, and Ransom began to run faster, paddle whirling in his hands as he tried to gain enough momentum to sweep some of this along with him. Exhausted by the need to keep up a brisk trot he tripped on to his knees, then stood up and raced after the pool as it approached the conveyor.

A fish flopped at his feet, twisting on the salt slope. Leaving it, Ransom rushed on after the pool, and caught up with it as it swirled through the metal legs. Lowering his head, he whipped the water with the paddle, and carried the pool over the slope into the next hollow.

Despite this slight gain, less than two-thirds of the original pool remained when he reached the lightship. To his left the sunlight was falling on the slopes of the salt-tips, lighting up the faces of the hills behind them, but Ransom ignored these intimations of warmth and colour. He steered the pool towards the small basin near the starboard bridge of the ship. This narrow tank, twenty yards long and ten wide, he had managed to preserve over the years by carrying stones and pieces of scrap metal down from the shore. Each day he beat the salt around them to a firm crust. The water was barely three inches deep, and a few edible kelp and water anemones, Ransom's sole source of vegetable food, floated limply at one end. Often Ransom had tried to breed fish in the pool, but the water was too saline and the fish invariably died within a few hours. In the reservoirs at the settlement, with their more dilute solutions, the fish lived for months. Unless he chose to live on dried kelp five days out of six, Ransom was obliged to go out almost every morning to trap and steal the sea.

He watched the pool as it slid into the tank like a tired snake, and then worked the wet bank with his paddle, squeezing the last water from the salt. The few fish swam up and down the steadying current, nibbling at the kelp. Counting them again, Ransom followed the line of old boiler tubes that ran from the tank to the fresh-water still next to his shack. He had roofed it in with pieces of metal plate from the cabins of the lightship, and with squares of old sacking. Opening the door, he listened for the familiar bubbling sounds, and then saw with annoyance that the flame under the boiler was set too low. The wastage of fuel, every ounce of which had to be scavenged with increasing difficulty from the vehicles buried beneath the shore, made him feel sick with frustration. A can of petrol sat on the floor. He poured some into the tank, then turned up the flame and adjusted it, careful, despite his annoyance, not to overheat the unit. Using this dangerous and unpredictable fuel, scores of stills had exploded over the years, killing or maiming their owners.

He examined the condenser for any leaks, and then raised the lid of the water receptacle. An inch of clear water lay in the pan. He decanted it carefully into an old whisky bottle, raising the funnel to his lips to catch the last intoxicating drops.

He walked over to the shack, touching his cheek, conscious that the bruised skin would show through his coarse stubble. Overhead the sunlight shone on the curving sternplates of the wrecked lightship, giving the port-holes a glassy opaque look like the eyes of a dead fish. In fact, this stranded leviathan, submerged beyond sight of the sea in this concentration of its most destructive element, had rotted as much as any whale would have done in ten years. Often Ransom entered the hulk, searching for pieces of piping or valve gear, but the engine room and gangways had rusted into grotesque hanging gardens of corroded metal.

Below the stern, partly sheltered from the prevailing easterly winds by the flat blade of the rudder, was Ransom's shack. He had built it from the rusty motor-car bodies he had hauled down from the shore and piled on top of one another. Its bulging shell, puffed out here and there by a car's bulbous nose or trunk, resembled the carapace of a cancerous turtle.

The central chamber, floored with wooden deck planks, was lit by a single fish-oil lamp when Ransom entered. Suspended from a chassis above, it swung slowly in the draughts moving through the cracks between the cars.

A small petrol stove, fitted with a crude flue, burned in the centre of the room. Two metal beds were drawn up against a table beside it. Lying on one of them, a patched blanket across her knees, was Judith Ransom. She looked up at Ransom, her dented temple casting an oblique shadow across the lace-like burn on her cheek. Since the accident she had made no further attempt to disguise the asymmetry of her face, and her greying hair was tied behind her neck in a simple knot.

'You're late,' she said. 'Did you catch anything?'

Ransom sat down and began to peel off the rubber suit. 'Five,' he told her. He rubbed his cheek painfully, aware that he and Judith now shared the same facial stigma. 'Three of them are quite big – there must be a lot to feed on out at sea. I had to leave one behind.'

'For heaven's sake, why?' Judith sat up, her face sharpening. 'We've got to give three to Grady, and you know he won't take small ones! That leaves us with only two for today!' She glanced about the shack with wavering desperation, as if hoping that in some magical way a small herring might materialize for her in each of the dingy corners. 'I can't understand you, Charles. You'll have to go out again tonight.'

Giving up the attempt to pull off his thigh-boots – made,

like his suit, from the inner tubes of car tyres — Ransom leaned back across the bed. 'Judith, I can't. I'm exhausted as it is.' Adopting the wheedling tone she herself had used, he went on: 'We don't want me to be ill again, do we?' He smiled at her encouragingly, turning his face from the lantern so that she would not see the weal. 'Anyway, they won't be going out again tonight. They brought in a huge lake of water.'

'They always do.' Judith gestured with a febrile hand. She had not yet recovered from Ransom's illness. The task of nursing him and begging for food had been bad enough, but faded into a trifle compared with the insecurity of being without the breadwinner for two weeks. 'Can't you go out to the sea and fish there? Why do you have to steal water all the time?'

Ransom let this reproof pass. He pressed his frozen hands to the stove. 'You can never reach the sea, can't you understand? There's nothing but salt all the way. Anyway, I haven't a net.'

'Charles, what's the matter with your face? Who did that?'

For a moment her indignant tone rallied Ransom's spirits, a display of that self-willed temper of old that had driven her from the Johnstone settlement five years earlier. It was this thin thread of independence that Ransom clung to, and he was almost glad of the injury for revealing it.

'We had a brief set-to with them. One of the paddle blades caught me.'

'My God! Whose, I'd like to know? Was it Jordan's?' When Ransom nodded she said with cold bitterness: 'One of these days someone will have his blood.'

'He was doing his job.'

'Rubbish. He picks on you deliberately.' She looked at Ransom critically, and then managed a smile. 'Poor Charles.'

Pulling his boots down to his ankles, Ransom crossed the hearth and sat down beside her, feeling the pale warmth inside her shawl. Her brittle fingers kneaded his shoulders and then brushed his greying hair from his forehead. Huddled beside her inside the blanket, one hand resting limply on her thin thighs, Ransom gazed around the drab interior of the shack. The decline in his life in the five years since Judith had come to live with him needed no underlining, but he realized that this was part of the continuous decline of all the beach settlements. It was true that he now had the task of feeding them both, and that Judith made little contribution to their survival, but she did at least guard their meagre fish and water stocks while he was away. Raids on the isolated outcasts had now become more frequent.

However, it was not this that held them together, but their awareness that only with each other could they keep alive some faint shadow of their former personalities, whatever their defects, and arrest the gradual numbing of sense and identity that was the unseen gradient of the dune limbo. Like all purgatories, the beach was a waiting-ground, the endless stretches of wet salt sucking away from them all but the hardest core of themselves. These tiny nodes of identity glimmered in the light of the limbo, the zone of nothingness that waited for them to dissolve and deliquesce like the crystals dried by the sun. During the first years, when Judith had lived with Hendry in the settlement, Ransom had noticed her becoming shrewish and sharp-tongued, and assumed this to mark the break-up of her personality. Later, when Hendry became the Reverend Johnstone's right-hand man, his association with Judith was a handicap. Her bodkin tongue and unpredictable ways made her intolerable to Johnstone's daughters and the other womenfolk.

She left the settlement of her own accord. After living

precariously in the old shacks among the salt-tips, she one day knocked on the door of Ransom's cabin. It was then that Ransom realized that in fact Judith was one of the few people on the beach to have survived intact. The cold and brine had merely cut away the soft tissues of convention and politeness. However bad-tempered and impatient, she was still herself.

Yet this stopping of the clock had gained them nothing. The beach was a zone without time, suspended in an endless interval as flaccid and enduring as the wet dunes themselves. Often Ransom remembered the painting by Tanguy which he had left behind in the houseboat. Its drained beaches, eroded of all associations, of all sense of time, in some ways seemed a photographic portrait of the salt world of the shore. But the similarity was misleading. On the beach, time was not absent but immobilized; what was new in their lives and relationships they could form only from the residues of the past, from the failures and omissions that persisted into the present like the wreckage and scrap metal from which they built their cabins.

Ransom looked down at Judith as she gazed into the stove. Despite the five years together, the five arctic winters and fierce summers when the salt banks gleamed like causeways of chalk, he felt few bonds between them. The success, if such a term could be used, of their present union, like its previous failure, had been decided by wholly impersonal considerations, above all by the zone of time in which they found themselves.

He stood up. 'I'll bring one of the fish down. We'll have some breakfast.'

'Can we spare it?'

'No. But perhaps there'll be a tidal wave tonight.'

Once every three or four years, in response to some distant submarine earthquake, a huge wave would inundate the coast. The third and last of these, some two years earlier, had swept across the salt flats an hour before dawn, reaching to the very margins of the beach. The hundreds of shacks and dwellings among the dunes had been destroyed by the waist-high water, the reservoir pools washed away in a few seconds. Staggering about in the sliding salt, they had watched everything they owned carried away. As the luminous water swilled around the wrecked ships, the exhausted beach-dwellers had climbed up on to the salt-tips and sat there until dawn.

Then, in the first light, they had seen a fabulous spectacle. The entire stretch of the draining salt flats was covered with the expiring forms of tens of thousands of stranded fish, every pool alive with crabs and shrimps. The ensuing blood-feast, as the gulls dived and screamed around the flashing spears, had rekindled the remaining survivors. For three weeks, led by the Reverend Johnstone, they had moved from pool to pool, and gorged themselves like beasts performing an obscene eucharist.

As Ransom walked over to the fish-tank he was thinking, not of this, but of the first great wave, some six months after their arrival. Then the tide had gathered for them a harvest of corpses. The thousands of bodies they had tipped into the sea after the final bloody battles on the beaches had come back to them, their drowned eyes and blanched faces staring from the shallow pools. The washed wounds, cleansed of all blood and hate, haunted them in their dreams. Working at night, they buried the bodies in deep graves below the first salt-tips. Sometimes Ransom would wake and go out into the darkness, half-expecting the washed bones to sprout through the salt below his feet.

Recently Ransom's memories of the corpses, repressed for so many years, had come back to him with added force. As he picked up his paddle and flicked one of the herrings on to the sand, he reflected that perhaps his reluctance to join the settlement stemmed from his identification of the fish with the bodies of the dead. However bitter his memories of the half-willing part he had played in the massacres, he now accepted that he would have to leave the solitary shack and join the Reverend Johnstone's small feudal world. At least the institutional relics and taboos would allay his memories in a way that he alone could not.

To Judith, as the fish browned in the frying pan, he said: 'Grady is going to join the settlement.'

'What? I don't believe it!' Judith brushed her hair down across her temple. 'He's always been such a lone wolf. Did he tell you himself?'

'Not exactly, but —'

'Then you're imagining it.' She divided the fish into two equal portions, steering the knife precisely down the midline with the casual skill of a surgeon. 'Jonathan Grady is his own master. He couldn't accept that crazy old clergyman and his mad daughters.'

Ransom chewed the flavourless steaks of white meat. 'He was talking about it while we waited for the tide. It was obvious what was on his mind — he's sensible enough to know we can't last out on our own much longer.'

'That's nonsense. We've managed so far.'

'But, Judith . . . we live like animals. The salt is shifting now; every day it carries the sea a few yards farther out.'

'Then we'll move along the coast. If we want to we can go a hundred miles.'

'Not now. There are too many blood feuds. It's an endless string of little communities, trapping their own small pieces of the sea and frightened of everyone else.' He picked at the shreds of meat around the fish's skull. 'I have a feeling Grady was warning me.'

'What do you mean?'

'If he joins the settlement he'll be one of Jordan's team.

He'll lead them straight here. In an obscure way I think he was telling me he'd enjoy getting his revenge.'

'For his father? But that was so far in the past. It was just one of those tragic accidents.'

'It wasn't. In fact, the more I think about it the more I'm convinced it was simply a kind of cold-blooded experiment, to see how detached from everyone else I was.' He shrugged. 'If we're going to join the settlement it would be best to get in before Grady does.'

Judith shook her head. 'Charles, if you go there it will be the end of you. You know that.'

An hour later, when she was asleep, Ransom left the cabin and went out into the cold morning light. The sun was overhead, but the dunes remained grey and lifeless, the shallow pools like clouded mirrors. Along the shore the rusting columns of the half-submerged stills rose into the air, their shafts casting striped shadows on the brilliant white slopes of the salt-tips. The hills beyond were bright with desert colours, but as usual Ransom turned his eyes from them.

He waited for five minutes to make sure that Judith remained asleep, then picked up his paddle and began to scoop the water from the tank beside the ship. Swept out by the broad blade, the water formed a pool some twenty feet wide, slightly larger than the one he had brought home that morning.

Propelling the pool in front of him, Ransom set off across the dunes, taking advantage of the slight slope that shelved eastwards from the beach. As he moved along he kept a careful watch on the shore. No one would attempt to rob him of so small a pool of water, but his departure might tempt some roving beachcomber to break into the shack. Here and there a set of footprints led up across the firmer salt, but otherwise the surface of the dunes was unmarked.

A mile away, towards the sea, a flock of gulls sat on the salt flats, but except for the pool of water scurrying along at Ransom's feet, nothing moved across the sky or land.

28

At the Settlement

Like a broken-backed lizard, the derelict conveyor crossed the dunes, winding off towards the hidden sea. Ransom changed course as he approached it, and set off over the open table of shallow salt-basins that extended eastwards along the coast. He moved in and out of the swells, following the long gradients that carried the pool under its own momentum. His erratic course also concealed his original point of departure. Half a mile ahead, when he passed below a second conveyor, a stout bearded man in a fur jacket watched him from one of the gantries, honing a whale-bone spear. Ransom ignored him and continued on his way.

In the distance a semi-circle of derelict freighters rose from the salt flats. Around them, like the hovels erected against the protective walls of a medieval fortress, was a clutter of small shacks and outbuildings. Some, like Ransom's, were built from the bodies of old cars salvaged from the beach, but others were substantial wood and metal huts, equipped with doors and glass windows, joined together by companion-ways of galvanized iron. Grey smoke lifted from the chimneys, conveying an impression of warmth and industry. A battery of ten large stills on the foreshore discharged its steam towards the distant hills.

A wire drift fence enclosed the settlement. As Ransom approached the western gate he could see the open surfaces of the water reservoirs and breeding tanks. Each was some two hundred feet long, buttressed by embankments of sand and shingle. A team of men, heads down in the cold sunlight, were working silently in one of the tanks, watched from the bank by an overseer holding a stave. Although three hundred people lived together in the settlement, no one moved around the central compound. As Ransom knew from his previous visits, the settlement's only activity was work.

Ransom steered his pool over to the gateway, where a group of huts gathered around the watch-tower. Two women sat in a doorway, rocking an anaemic child. At various points along the perimeter of the settlement a few sub-communities had detached themselves from the main compound, either because they were the original occupants of the site or were too lazy or unreliable to fit into the puritan communal life. However, all of them possessed some special skill with which they paid for their places.

Bullen, the gatekeeper, who peered at Ransom from his sentry-box below the watch-tower, carved the paddles used by the sea-trappers. In long racks by the huts the narrow blades, wired together from pieces of whale-bone, dried in the sunlight. In return, Bullen had been granted proprietary rights to the gateway. A tall, hunchbacked man with a sallow face, he watched Ransom suspiciously, then walked slowly across the water-logged hollows below the tower.

'Back again?' he said. Despite the infrequency of his visits, Ransom seemed to worry him in some obscure way. This was a symptom of the general withdrawal of the settlement from the world outside. He pointed down at Ransom's pool with a paddle. 'What have you got there?'

'I want to see Captain Hendry,' Ransom said.

Bullen released the gate. As Ransom steered the pool forwards Bullen held it back with his paddle. Wearily,

Ransom swept several bladefuls of the water into the basin by the tower. Usually Bullen would have expected a pair of small herring at the least, but from his brief glance at Ransom's appearance he seemed to accept that these few gallons of water were the limit of his wealth.

As the gate closed behind him, Ransom set off towards the compound. The largest of the freighters, its bows buried under the salt, formed the central tower of the settlement. Part of the starboard side, facing the shore, had been dismantled and a series of two- and three-storey cabins were built on to the decks. The stern castle of the ship, jutting high into the air, was topped by a large whale-bone cross. This was the settlement's chapel. The port-holes and windows had been replaced by crude stained glass images of biblical scenes, in which some local craftsman had depicted Christ and his disciples surrounded by leaping sharks and sea-horses.

The settlement's preoccupation with the sea and its creatures could be seen at a glance. Outside every hut dozens of small fish dried on trestle tables or hung from the eaves. Larger fish, groupers and sharks that had strayed into the shallow water, were suspended from the rails of the ships, while an immense swordfish, the proudest catch of the settlement and the Reverend Johnstone's choice of a militant symbol to signify its pride, was tied to the whale-bone mast and hung below the cross, its huge blade pointed heavenwards.

On the seaward side of the ships a second team of men was working in one of the tanks, bending in the cold water as they harvested the edible kelp. Swathed in rubber tubing, they looked like primitive divers experimenting with makeshift suits.

Directly below the gangway of the freighter half a dozen round basins had been cut in the salt-dunes, temporary storage tanks for people moving with their water up and down the coast. Ransom steered his pool into the second of them, next to a visiting fisherman selling his wares to one of the foremen. The two men argued together, stepping down into the water and feeling the plump plaice and soles.

Ransom drove his paddle into the sand by his pool. Some of the water had been lost on the way, and there was barely enough to cover the floor of the basin.

He called up to the look-out on the bridge: 'Is Captain Hendry aboard? Ransom to see him.'

The man came down the companion-way to the deck, and beckoned Ransom after him. They walked past the boarded-up port-holes. Unpainted for ten years, the hulk was held together by little more than the tatters of rust. The scars of shell-fire marked the decks and stanchions – the freighter, loaded with fresh water and supplies, had been stormed by the insurgents breaking out from the rear areas of the beach, and then shelled from the destroyer now reclining among the dunes, a hundred yards away. Through one of these rents, gaping like an empty flower in the deck overhead, Ransom could see an old surplice drying in the sun.

'Wait here. I'll see the Captain.'

Ransom leaned on the rail, looking down at the yard below. An old woman in a black shawl chopped firewood with an axe, while another straightened the kelp drying on a frame in the sunlight. The atmosphere in the settlement was drab and joyless, like that of an early pilgrim community grimly held together on the edge of some northern continent. Partly this was due to the sense of remorse still felt by the survivors – the spectres of the thousands who had been killed on the beaches, or driven out in herds to die in the sea, haunted the bitter salt. But it also reflected the gradual attrition of life, the slow reduction of variety and movement as the residues of their past lives, the only materials left to them, sank into the sterile dunes. This sense of diminishing possibility, of the erosion of all time and space beyond the flaccid sand and draining beaches, numbed Ransom's mind.

'The Captain will see you.'

Ransom followed the man into the ship. The nautical terminology – there were a dozen captains, including Hendry, Jordan and the Reverend Johnstone, a kind of ex-officio rear-admiral – was a hangover from the first years when the nucleus of the original settlement had lived in the ship. The freighter sat where she had been sunk in the shallow water, the waves breaking her up, until the slopes of salt produced by the distillation units had driven the water back into the sea. At this stage thousands of emigrants were living in the cars and shacks on the beaches, and the distillation units, run by the citizens' co-operatives that had taken over from the military after the break-out battles, were each producing tons of salt every day. The large freighter had soon been inundated.

'Well, what have you brought now?' Seated at his desk in the purser's cabin, Hendry looked up as Ransom came in. Waving Ransom into a chair, he peered down the columns of a leather-bound log-book which he used as a combined ledger and diary. In the intervening years all trace of Hendry's former quiet humour had gone, and only the residue of the conscientious policeman remained. Dour and efficient, but so dedicated to securing the minimum subsistence level for the settlement that he could no longer visualize anything above that meagre line, he summed up for Ransom all the dangers and confinements of their limbo.

'Judith sends her regards, Captain,' Ransom began, trying to force a little brightness into his manner. 'How's the baby coming along?'

Hendry gestured with his pen. 'As well as can be expected.'

'Would you like some water for it? I have some outside.

I was going to hand it over to the settlement, but I'd be delighted to give you and Julia the first cut.'

Hendry glanced cannily at Ransom, as if suspecting that this harmless outcast, however incompetent, might have stumbled on some Elysian spring. 'What water is this? I didn't know you had so much you were giving it away.'

'It isn't mine to give,' Ransom said piously. 'The poachers were out again last night, stealing Jordan's catch as it came in. I found this pool near the channel this morning.'

Hendry stood up. 'Let's have a look at it.' He led the way out on to the deck. 'Where is it? *That* one down there?' Shaking his head, he started back for his cabin. 'Doctor, what are you playing at?'

Ransom caught up with him. 'Judith and I have been talking it over seriously, Captain . . . it's been selfish of us living alone, but now we're prepared to join the settlement. You'll soon need all the help you can get to bring in the sea.'

Hendry hesitated, embarrassed by Ransom's pleading. 'We're not short of water.'

'Perhaps that's true, in the immediate sense, but a year or two from now – we've got to think ahead.'

Hendry nodded to himself. 'That's good advice.' He turned in the door to his cabin. For a moment the old Hendry glimmered faintly in his eyes. 'Thanks for the offer of the water. Look, Charles, you wouldn't like it in the settlement. The people have given too much. If you came here they'd drain you away.'

Reflectively he patted the carcass of a small shark hanging in the sun outside the cabin. The shrivelled white face gaped sightlessly at Ransom.

29

The Stranded Neptune

Resting on the rail, Ransom pulled himself together. Much as he despised himself for trying to ingratiate his way into the settlement, he realized that there were no other means. However, even these appeals to past sentiments were wearing thin. Hendry's prompt refusal meant that he was acting on a decision already reached by the other captains.

Yet a sense of inner conviction still sustained Ransom. The fleeting sunlight warmed his face, and he looked down at the drab hutments below, almost glad that he was not coming to live out the rest of his life there. Somewhere, God alone knew how, he would find a way out of his present purgatory. This vague feeling had kept him going since the day he arrived at the beach, as if he had never fully believed in the reality of the sea. At a time of drought, water was the last yardstick to use. Their ten years at the coast had proved that much.

The look-out stood by the gangway, watching Ransom as he drummed on the rail. Ransom went over to him. 'Where's Captain Jordan? Is he here?'

The man shook his head. 'He's over in the cliffs. He won't be back till afternoon.'

Ransom looked back at the distant hills, debating whether to wait for Jordan, the last person who could influence his admission to the settlement. Almost every afternoon Jordan went out to the hills above the beach, disappearing among the sand-dunes that spilled through the ravines. Ransom guessed that he was visiting the grave of his foster-father, Mr Jordan. The old negro had died a few days after their arrival at the beach, and Philip had buried him somewhere among the dunes.

As he stepped past the look-out, the man said softly: 'Miss Vanessa wants to see you.'

Nodding to him, Ransom glanced up and down the deserted hulk of the ship, and then crossed to the port side. The look-out's feet rang softly on the metal rails of the bridge, but otherwise this side of the ship was silent.

Ransom walked along the empty deck. A rusty companion-way led to the boat-deck above. Most of the lifeboats had been smashed to splinters in the bombardment, but the line of officers' cabins was still intact. In one of these small cubicles behind the bridge, Vanessa Johnstone lived by herself.

Ransom reached the companion-way, then stopped to glance through a damaged ventilator. Below was the central chamber of the ship. This long, high-ceilinged room had been formed when the floor dividing the passenger lounge from the dining-room below had rusted out. It was now the Reverend Johnstone's combined vestry and throne-chamber.

A few oil-lamps flared from brackets on the wall, and cast a flickering submarine glow on to the ceiling. The shadows of the torn deck braces danced like ragged spears. The floor of the chamber was covered with mats of dried kelp to keep out the cold. In the centre, almost below Ransom, the Reverend Johnstone sat in an armchair mounted in the bow section of his old motor-launch, the craft from which Johnstone had led the first assault on the freighter. The conch-like bowl, with its striped white timbers, was fastened to the dais of the bandstand. On the floor beside him were his daughters, Julia and Frances, with two or three other women, murmuring into their shawls and playing with a baby swaddled in rags of lace.

Looking down at the two daughters, Ransom found it difficult to believe that only ten years had elapsed since their arrival at the beach. Their faces had been puffed up by the endless diet of herring and fish-oil, and they had the thickened cheekbones and moon-chins of Eskimo squaws. Sitting beside their father, shawls over their heads, they reminded Ransom of a pair of sleek, watchful madonnas. For some reason he was convinced that he owned his exclusion from the settlement to those two women. The proponents above all of the status quo, guardians and presiding angels of the dead time, perhaps they regarded him as a disruptive influence, someone who had managed to preserve himself against the dunes and salt flats.

Certainly their senile father, the Reverend Johnstone, could now be discounted as an influence. Sitting like a stranded Neptune in the bowels of this salt-locked wreck, far out of sight of the sea, he drooled and wavered on his throne of blankets, clutching at his daughters' hands. He had been injured in the bombardment, and the right side of his face was pink and hairless. The grey beard tufting from his left cheek gave him the appearance of a demented Lear, grasping back at the power he had given to his daughters. The difference was that Johnstone no longer knew where that power lay. His head bobbed about, and Ransom guessed that for two or three years he had been almost blind. The confined world of the settlement was limited by his own narrowing vision, and sinking into a rigid matriarchy dominated by his two daughters.

If any escape lay for Ransom, only the third daughter could provide it. As he reached the deserted boat-deck of the freighter, Ransom felt that the climb had carried him in all senses above the drab world of the settlement.

'Charles!' Vanessa Johnstone was lying in her bunk in

the cold cabin, gazing through the open door at the gulls on the rail. Her black hair lay in a single coil on her pale breast. Her plain face was as smooth and unmarked as when she sat by the window of her attic bedroom in Hamilton. Ransom closed the door and seated himself on the bunk beside her, taking her hands. She seized them tightly, greeting him with her eager smile. 'Charles, you're here —'

'I came to see Hendry, Vanessa.' She embraced his shoulders with her cold hands. Her blood always seemed chilled, but it ran with the quicksilver of time, its clear streams darting like the fish he had chased at dawn. The cold air in the cabin and her white skin, like the washed shells gleaming on the beaches in the bright winter sun, made his mind run again.

'Hendry — why?'

'I . . .' Ransom hesitated. He had visited Vanessa at intervals during the past years, when her illness seemed about to return, but he was frightened of at last committing himself to her. If she opened his way to the settlement he would be cast with Vanessa for ever. 'I want to bring Judith here and join the settlement. Hendry wasn't very keen.'

'But Charles —' Vanessa shook her head, one hand touching his cheek. 'You can't come here. It's out of all question.'

'Why?' Ransom took her wrists, surprised by her answer. 'You both assume that. It's a matter of survival now. The sea is so far out —'

'The sea! Forget the sea!' Vanessa regarded Ransom with her sombre eyes. 'If you come here, Charles, it will be the end for you. All day you'll be raking the salt from the boilers.'

Half an hour later, as he lay beside her in the bunk, the chilled air from the sea blowing over him through the porthole, he asked: 'What else is there, Vanessa?'

He waited as she lay back against the white pillow, the cold air in the cabin turning the black spirals of her hair. 'Do you know, Vanessa?'

Her eyes were on the gulls high above the ship, picking at the body of the great swordfish hanging from the mast.

30

The Sign of the Crab

High above the dunes, in the tower of the lightship, Ransom watched Philip Jordan walking among the salt-tips on the shore. Silhouetted against the white slopes, his tall figure seemed stooped and preoccupied as he picked his way slowly along the stony path. He passed behind one of the tips, and then climbed the sand-slopes that reached down from the ravines between the hills, a cloth bag swinging from his hand.

Sheltered from the wind by the fractured panels of the glass cupola, Ransom for a moment enjoyed the play of sunlight on the sand-dunes and on the eroded faces of the cliff. The coastal hills now marked the edges of the desert that stretched in a continuous table across the continent, a wasteland of dust and ruined towns, but there was always more colour and variety here than in the drab world of the salt flats. In the morning the seams of quartz would melt with light, pouring like liquid streams down the faces of the cliffs, the sand in the ravines turning into frozen fountains. In the afternoon the colours would mellow again, the shadows searching out the hundreds of caves and aerial grottoes, until the evening light, shining from beyond the cliffs to the west, illuminated the whole coastline like an enormous ruby lantern, glowing through the casements of the cave-mouths as if lit by some subterranean fire.

When Philip Jordan had gone, Ransom climbed down

the stairway and stepped out on to the deck of the light-ship. Beyond the rail a single herring circled the tank — Grady had come to demand his due while Ransom was at the settlement — and the prospect of the dismal meal to be made of the small fish made Ransom turn abruptly from the shack. Judith was asleep, exhausted by her altercation with Grady. Below him the deck shelved towards the salt-dunes sliding across the beach. Crossing the rail, Ransom walked off towards the shore, avoiding the shallow pools of brine disturbed by the wind.

The salt slopes became firmer. He climbed up towards the salt-tips, which rose against the hills like white pyra-mids. The remains of a large still jutted through the surface of the slope, the corroded valve-gear decorating the rusty shaft. Ransom stepped across the brown shell of a metal hut, his feet sinking through the lace-like iron, then climbed past a pile of derelict motor-car bodies half-buried in salt. When he reached the tips he searched the ground for Philip Jordan's footprints, but the dry salt was covered with dozens of tracks left by the sledges pulled by the quarry workers.

Beyond the salt-tips stretched the open ground that had once been the coastal shelf. The original dunes had been buried under the salt washed up from the beach during the storms, and by the drifts of sand and dust blown down from the hills. The grey sandy soil, in which a few clumps of grass gained a precarious purchase, was strewn with half-buried pieces of ironwork and metal litter. Somewhere beneath Ransom's feet were the wrecks of thousands of cars and trucks. Isolated bonnets and windscreens poked through the sand, and sections of barbed-wire fencing rose into the air for a few yards. Here and there the roof-timbers of one of the beach-side villas sheltered the remains of an old hearth.

Some four hundred yards to his right was the mouth of

the drained river, along which he had first reached the shore ten years earlier. Partly hidden by the quarry workings, the banks had been buried under the thousands of tons of sand and loose rock slipping down into the empty bed from the adjacent hills. Ransom skirted the edges of the quarry, making his way carefully through the wasteland of old chassis and fenders thrown to one side.

The entrance to the quarry sloped to his left, the ramp leading down to the original beach. In the face of the quarry were the half-excavated shells of a dozen cars and trailers, embedded in the gritty sand like the intact bodies of armoured saurians. Here, at the quarry, the men from the settlement were digging out the car shells, picking through them for tyres, seats and rags of clothing.

Beyond the quarry the dunes gave way to a small hollow, from which protruded the faded gilt roof of an old fairground booth. The striped wooden awning hung over the silent horses of the merry-go-round, frozen like unicorns on their spiral shafts. Next to it was another of the booths, a line of washing strung from its decorated eaves. Ransom followed one of the pathways cut through the dunes to this little dell. Here Mrs Quilter lived out of sight of the sea and shore, visited by the quarry-workers and womenfolk of the settlement, for whom she practised her mild necromancy and fortune-telling. Although frowned upon by the Reverend Johnstone and his captains, these visits across the dunes served a useful purpose, introducing into their sterile lives, Ransom believed, those random elements, that awareness of chance and time, without which they would soon have lost all sense of identity.

As he entered the dell, Mrs Quilter was sitting in the doorway of her booth, darning a shawl. At the sound of footsteps she put away her needle and closed the lower half of the painted door, then kicked it open again when she recognized Ransom. In the ten years among the dunes she had barely aged. If anything her beaked face was softer, giving her the expression of a quaint and amiable owl. Her small body was swathed in layers of coloured fabrics stitched together from the oddments salvaged by the quarry-workers – squares of tartan blanket, black velvet and faded corduroy, ruffed with strips of embroidered damask.

Outside the door was a large jar of fish-oil. A dozen herrings, part of her recent take, dried in the sun. On the slopes around her, lines of shells and conches had been laid out in the sand to form pentacles and crescents.

Dusting the sand off the shells as Ransom approached was Catherine Austen. She looked up, greeting him with a nod. Despite the warm sunlight in the hollow, she had turned up the leather collar of her fleece-lined jacket, hiding her lined face. Her self-immersed eyes reminded Ransom of the first hard years she had spent with the old woman, eking out their existence among the wrecks of the motor-cars. The success of their present relationship – both had the same fading red hair, which made them seem like mother and daughter – was based on their absolute dependence on each other and rigorous exclusion of everyone else.

On the sloping sand Catherine had set out the signs of the zodiac, the dotted lines outlining the crab, ram and scorpion.

'That looks professional,' Ransom commented. 'What's my horoscope for the day?'

'When were you born? Which month?'

'Cathy!' Mrs Quilter waved her fist at Ransom from her booth. 'That'll be a herring, doctor. Don't give him charity, dear.'

Catherine nodded at the old woman, then turned to Ransom with a faint smile. Her strong, darkly tanned face was hardened by the spray and wind. 'Which month? Don't tell me you've forgotten?'

'Early June,' Ransom said. 'Aquarius?'

'Cancer,' Catherine corrected. 'The sign of the crab, doctor, the sign of deserts. I wish I'd known.'

'Fair enough,' Ransom said. They walked past the merry-go-round. He raised his hand to one of the horses and touched its eyes. 'Deserts? Yes, I'll take the rest as read.'

'But which desert, doctor? There's a question for you.'

Ransom shrugged. 'Does it matter? It seems we have a knack of turning everything we touch into sand and dust. We've even sown the sea with its own salt.'

'That's a despairing view, doctor. I hope you give your patients a better prognosis.'

Ransom looked down into her keen eyes. As she well knew, he had no patients. During the early years at the beach he had tended hundreds of sick and wounded, but almost all of them had died, from exposure and malnutrition. By now he was regarded as a pariah by the people of the settlement, on the principle that a person who needed a doctor would soon die.

'I haven't got any patients,' he said quietly. 'They refuse to let me treat them. Perhaps they prefer your brand of reassurance.' He looked around at the hills above. 'For a doctor there's no greater failure. Did you see Philip Jordan? About half an hour ago?'

'He went by. I've no idea where.'

She followed a few paces behind him as he took one of the pathways out of the dell, almost as if she wanted to come with him. Then she turned and went back to Mrs Quilter.

For half an hour Ransom climbed the dunes, wandering in and out of the foot-hills below the cliffs. Old caves studded the base, glass windows and doors of tin sheeting let into their mouths, but the dwellings had been abandoned for years. The sand retained something of the sun's warmth, and for ten minutes Ransom lay down and played with the tags of waste paper caught in its surface. Behind him the slopes rose to a smooth bluff a hundred feet above the dunes, the headland jutting out over the surrounding hills. Ransom climbed up its flank, hoping that from here he would see Philip Jordan when he returned to the settlement.

Reaching the bluff, he sat down and scanned the beach below. In the distance lay the shore, the endless banks of salt undulating towards the sea. The wrecked freighters in the settlement were grouped together like ships in a small port. Ignoring them, Ransom looked out over the bed of the river. For more than half a mile the estuary was overrun by dunes and rock-slides. Gradually the surface cleared to form a white deck, scattered with stones and small rocks, the dust blown between the clumps of grass.

Exploring the line of the bank, Ransom noticed that a small valley led off among the rocks and ravines. Like the river, the valley was filled with sand and dust, the isolated walls of the ruined houses on the slopes half-covered by the dunes.

In the slanting light Ransom could clearly see the line of foot-prints newly cut in the powdery flank. They led straight up to the ruins of a large villa, crossing the edge of partly excavated road around the valley.

As Ransom made his way down from the bluff he saw Philip Jordan emerge briefly behind a wall, then disappear down a flight of steps.

31

The White Lion

Five minutes later, as Ransom climbed the slope to what he guessed was the old negro's secret grave, a rock hurtled through the air past his head. He crouched down and watched the rock, the size of a fist, bound away off the sand.

'Philip!' he shouted into the sunlight. 'It's Ransom!'

Philip Jordan's narrow face appeared at the edge of the road. 'Go away, Ransom,' he called brusquely. 'Get back to the beach.' He picked up a second stone. 'Ive already let you off once today.'

Ransom held his footing in the shifting sand. He pointed to the ruined villa. 'Philip, don't forget who brought him here. But for me he wouldn't be buried at all.'

Philip Jordan stepped forward to the edge of the road. Holding the rock loosely in one hand, he watched Ransom begin the climb up to him. He raised the rock above his head. 'Ransom . . . !' he called warningly.

Ransom stopped again. Despite Philip Jordan's advantages in strength and years, Ransom found himself seizing at this final confrontation. As he edged up the slope, remembering the knife hidden in his right boot, he knew that Philip Jordan was at last repaying him for all the help Ransom had given to the river-borne waif fifteen years earlier. No one could incur such an obligation without settling it to the full one day in its reverse coin. But above all, perhaps, Philip saw in Ransom's face a likeness of his true father, the wandering fisher-captain who had called him from the river-bank and from whom he had run away for a second time.

Ransom climbed upwards, feeling with his feet for spurs of buried rock. His eyes watched the stone in Philip's hand, shining in the sunlight against the open sky.

Standing on a ledge twenty feet above the road, unaware of the scene below, was a thin, long-bodied animal with a ragged mane. Its grey skin was streaked white by the dust, the narrow flanks scarred with thorn marks, and for a moment Ransom failed to recognize it. Then he raised his hand and pointed, as the beast gazed out at the wet salt flats and the distant sea.

'Philip,' he whispered hoarsely. 'There, on the ledge!'

Philip Jordan glanced over his shoulder, then dropped to one knee and hurled the stone from his hand. As the piece burst into a dozen fragments at its feet, the small lion leapt frantically to one side. With its tail down it bolted away across the rocky slopes, legs carrying it in a blur of dust.

As Ransom clambered up on to the road he felt Philip's hand on his arm. The young man was still watching the lion as it raced along the dry river-bed. His hand was shaking, less with fear than some deep unrestrainable excitement.

'What's that – a white panther?' he asked thickly, his eyes following the distant plume of dust vanishing among the dunes.

'A lion,' Ransom said. 'A small lion. It looked hungry.' He pulled Philip's shoulder. 'Philip! Do you realize—? You remember Quilter and the zoo? The lion must have come all the way from Mount Royal! It means. . .' He broke off, the dust in his throat and mouth. A feeling of immense relief surged through him, washing away the pain and bitterness of the past ten years.

Philip Jordan waited for Ransom to catch his breath. 'I

know, doctor. It means there's water between here and
Mount Royal.'

A concrete ramp curved down behind the wall into the
basement garage of the house. The dust and rock-falls had
been cleared away, and a palisade of wooden stakes carefully wired together held back the drifts of sand.

Still light-headed, Ransom pointed to the smooth concrete, and to the fifty yards of clear roadway excavated
from the side of the valley. 'You've worked hard, Philip.
The old man would be proud of you.'

Philip Jordan took a key from the wallet on his belt
and unlocked the door. 'Here we are, doctor.' He gestured
Ransom forward. 'What do you think of it?'

Standing in the centre of the garage, its chromium grille
gleaming in the shadows, was an enormous black hearse.
The metal roof and body had been polished to a mirror-like
brilliance, and the hubcaps shone like burnished shields.
To Ransom, who for years had seen nothing but damp rags
and rusting iron, whose only homes had been a succession
of dismal hovels, the limousine seemed like an embalmed
fragment of an unremembered past.

'Philip,' he said. 'It's magnificent, of course . . .' Cautiously he walked around the huge black vehicle. Three
of the tyres were intact and pumped up, but the fourth
had been removed and the axle jacked on to a set of wooden
blocks. Unable to see into the glowing leatherwork and
mahogany interior, he wondered if the old negro's body
reposed in a coffin in the back. Perhaps Philip, casting his
mind back to the most impressive memories of his childhood, had carried with him all these years a grotesque
image of the ornate hearses he had seen rolling around
Mount Royal on their way to the cemeteries.

He peered through the rear window. The wooden bier
was empty, the chromium tapers clean and polished.

'Philip, where is he? Old Mr Jordan?'

Philip gestured off-handedly. 'Miles from here. He's buried in a cave above the sea. This is what I wanted to show you, doctor. What do you think of it?'

Collecting himself, Ransom said: 'But they told me, everyone thought – all this time you've been coming here, Philip? To this . . . car?'

Philip unlocked the driver's door. 'I found it five years ago. You understand I couldn't drive, there wasn't any point then, but it gave me an idea. I started looking after it, a year ago I found a couple of new tyres . . .' He spoke quickly, eager to bring Ransom up to date, as if the discovery and renovation of the hearse were the only events of importance to have taken place in the previous ten years.

'What are you going to do with it?' Ransom asked. He opened the driver's door. 'Can I get in?'

'Of course.' Philip wound down the window when Ransom was seated. 'As a matter of fact, doctor, I want you to start it for me.'

The ignition keys were in the dashboard. Ransom switched on. He looked around to see Philip watching him in the half-light, his dark face, like an intelligent savage's, filled with a strange child-like hope. Wondering how far he was still a dispensable tool, Ransom said: 'I'll be glad to, Philip. I understand how you feel about the car. It's been a long ten years, the car takes one back . . .'

Philip smiled, showing a broken tooth and the white scar below his left eye. 'But please carry on. The tank is full of fuel, there's oil in the engine, and the radiator is full.'

Nodding, Ransom pressed the starter. As he expected, nothing happened. He pressed the starter several times, then released the hand-brake and moved the gear lever through its sequence. Philip Jordan shook his head, only a faint look of disappointment on his face.

Ransom handed the keys to him. He stepped from the car. 'It won't go, Philip, you understand that, don't you? The battery is flat, and all the electrical wiring will have corroded. You'll never start it, not in a hundred years. I'm sorry, it's a beautiful car.'

With a shout, Philip Jordan slammed his foot at the half-open door, kicking it into the frame. The muscles of his neck and cheeks were knotted like ropes, as if all the frustration of the past years were tearing his face apart. With a wrench he ripped the windscreen wiper from its pinion, then drummed his fists on the bonnet, denting the polished metal.

'It's got to go, doctor, if I have to push it myself all the way!' He threw Ransom aside, then bent down and put his shoulder to the frame. With animal energy he drove the car forward on its wheels. There was a clatter as the blocks toppled to the floor, and the back axle and bumper dropped on to the concrete. The car sagged downwards, its body panels groaning. Philip raced around it, pulling at the doors and fenders with his strong hands.

Ransom stepped out into the sunlight and waited there. Ten minutes later Philip came out, head bowed, his right hand bleeding across his wrist.

Ransom took his arm. 'We don't need the car, Philip. Mount Royal is only a hundred miles away, we can walk it comfortably in two or three weeks. The river will take us straight there.'

Part Three

32

The Illuminated River

Like a bleached white bone, the flat deck of the river stretched away to the north. At its margins, where the remains of the stone embankment formed a ragged windbreak, the dunes had gathered together in high drifts, and these defined the winding course of the drained bed. Beyond the dunes was the desert floor, littered with fragments of dried mud like shards of pottery. At intervals the stump of a tree marked the distance of a concealed ridge from the river, or a metal windmill, its rusty vanes held like a cipher above the empty wastes, stood guard over a dried-up creek. In the coastal hills, the upper slopes of the valley had flowered with a few clumps of hardy gorse sustained by the drifts of spray, but ten miles from the sea the desert was arid, the surface crumbling beneath the foot into a fine white powder. The metal refuse scattered about the dunes provided the only floral decoration – twisted bedsteads rose like clumps of desert thorns, water pumps and farm machinery formed angular sculptures, the dust spuming from their vanes in the light breeze.

Revived by the spring sunlight, the small party moved at a steady pace along the drained bed. In the three days since setting out they had covered twenty miles, walking unhurriedly over the lanes of firmer sand that wound along the bed. In part their rate of progress was dictated by Mrs Quilter, who insisted on walking a few miles each morning.

During the afternoon she agreed to sit on the cart, half asleep under the awning, while Ransom and Catherine Austen took turns at pushing it with Philip Jordan. With its large wooden wheels and light frame the cart was easy to move. Inside its locker were the few essentials of their expedition – a tent and blankets, a case of smoked herring and edible kelp, and half a dozen large cans of water, enough, Ransom estimated, for three weeks. Unless they found water during the journey to Mount Royal they would have to give up and turn back before reaching the city, but they all tacitly accepted that they would not be returning to the coast.

The appearance of the lion convinced Ransom that there was water within twenty or thirty miles of the coast, probably released from a spring or underground river. Without this, the lion would not have survived, and its hasty retreat up the river indicated that the drained bed had been its route to the coast. They came across no spoors of the creature, but each morning their own footprints around the camp were soon smoothed over by the wind. None the less Ransom and Jordan kept a sharp watch for the animal, their hands never far from the spears fastened to the sides of the cart.

Ransom gathered from Mrs Quilter that the three of them had been preparing for the journey for the past year. At no time had there been any formal plan or route, but merely a shared sense of the need to retrace their steps towards the city and the small town by the drained lake. Mrs Quilter was obviously looking for her son, convinced that he was still alive somewhere in the ruins of the city.

Philip Jordan's motives, like Catherine's, were more concealed. Whether, in fact, he was searching for his father, Jonas, or for the painted houseboat he had shared with the old negro, Ransom could not discover. He guessed that Mrs Quilter had sensed these undercurrents during Philip's visits to her booth, and then played on them, knowing that she and Catherine could never make the journey on their own. When Philip revealed the whereabouts of the car to her, Mrs Quilter had needed no further persuasion.

Ironically, the collapse of the plan to drive in style to Mount Royal in the magnificently appointed hearse had returned Ransom to her favour.

'It was a grand car, doctor,' she told him for the tenth time, as they finished an early lunch under the shade of the cart. 'That would have shown my old Quilty, wouldn't it?' She gazed into the distant haze, this vision of the prodigal mother's return hovering over the dunes. 'Now I'll be sitting up in this old cart like a sack of potatoes.'

'He'll be just as glad to see you, Mrs Quilter.' Ransom buried the remains of their meal in the sand. 'Anyway, the car would have broken down within ten miles.'

'Not if you'd been driving, doctor. I remember how you brought us here.' Mrs Quilter leaned back against the wheel. 'You just started those cars with a press of your little finger.'

Philip Jordan paced across to her, wary of this swing in her loyalties. 'Mrs Quilter, the battery was flat. It had been there for ten years.'

Mrs Quilter brushed this aside. 'Batteries . . . ! Help me up, would you, doctor. We'd best be pushing this cart on a bit more. Perhaps Philip will find us an old donkey somewhere.'

They lifted her up under the awning. Ransom leaned againt the shaft next to Catherine, while Philip Jordan patrolled the bank fifty yards ahead, spear in hand. Mrs Quilter's upgrading of Ransom's status had not yet extended to Catherine Austen. She pushed away steadily at her handle, her leather jacket fastened by its sleeves around her strong shoulders. When the wheel on Ransom's side lodged itself in the cracked surface, she chided him:

'Come on, doctor – or do you want to sit up there with Mrs Quilter?'

Ransom bided his time, and remembered when he had first seen Catherine in the zoo at Mount Royal, exciting the lions in the cages. Since leaving them she had been subdued and guarded, but already he could feel her reviving again, drawn to the empty savannahs and the quickening pulse of the desert cats.

They moved forward along the river, as Mrs Quilter drowsed under the awning, her violet silks ruffled like half-furled sails in the warm air. Ahead of them the river continued its serpentine course between the dunes. Its broad surface, nearly three hundred yards wide, reflected the sunlight like a chalk deck. In the centre the draining water had grooved the surface, and it resembled the weathered dusty hide of an albino elephant. The wheels broke the crust, and their footsteps churned the dust into soft plumes that drifted away on the air behind them. Everywhere the sand was mingled with the fine bones of small fish, the white flakes of mollusc shells.

Once or twice Ransom glanced over his shoulder towards the coast, glad to see that the dust obscured his view of the hills above the beach. Already he had forgotten the long ten years on the salt flats, the winter nights crouched among the draining brine pools, and the running battles with the men of the settlement. He had left Judith without warning, but Philip Jordan told him she would be accepted at the settlement. Ironically, Philip also told Ransom that there had been no agreed decision to exclude him from the settlement. However, Hendry had been acting on a common instinct, the shared feeling that Ransom by his very sense of failure would remind each of them of everything they themselves had lost.

The river turned to the north-east. They passed the remains of a line of wharfs. Stranded lighters, almost buried under the sand, lay beside them, their grey hulks blanched and empty. A group of ruined warehouses stood on the bank, single walls rising into the air with their upper windows intact. A road ran towards the hills across the alluvial plain, its direction marked by a line of telegraph poles.

At this point the river had been dredged and widened. They passed more launches and river-craft, half-submerged under the sand-hills. Ransom stopped and let the others move on ahead. He looked at the craft beached around him. Shadowless in the vertical sunlight, their rounded forms seemed to have been eroded of all but a faint residue of their original identities, like ghosts in a distant universe where drained images lay in the shallows of some lost time. The unvarying light and absence of all movement made Ransom feel that he was advancing across an inner landscape where the elements of the future stood around him like the objects in a still life, formless and without association.

They stopped by the hulk of a river steamer, a graceful craft with a tall white funnel, which had run aground in the centre of the channel. The deck was level with the surrounding sand. Ransom walked to the rail and stepped over it, then strolled across to the open doors of the saloon below the bridge. The dust lay over the floor and tables, its slopes cloaking the seats and corner upholstery.

Catherine and Philip Jordan climbed on to the bridge and looked out over the plain for any signs of movement. Two miles away the aluminium towers of a grain silo shone against the hills.

'Can you see anything?' Ransom called up. 'Hot springs should send up clouds of steam.'

Philip shook his head. 'Nothing, doctor.'

Ransom walked forward to the bows and sat down on the capstan. Lowering his head, he saw that its shadow lay across his hands. Cupping them together, he altered the outline of his skull, varying its shape and length. He noticed Mrs Quilter eyeing him curiously from her seat atop the cart.

'Doctor, that's a trick my Quilty had. You looked like him then. Poor lad, he was trying to straighten his head like everyone else's.'

Ransom crossed the rail and went over to her. On an impulse he reached up and held her hand. Small and round, its pulse fluttered faintly, like a trembling sparrow. Mrs Quilter gazed down at him with her vague eyes, her mind far away. Suddenly Ransom found himself hoping against all logic that they would discover Quilter somewhere.

'We'll find him, Mrs Quilter. He'll still be there.'

'It's a dream, doctor, just a dream, a woman's fancy. But I couldn't rest until I've tried.'

Ahead of them was a sharp bend in the river. A herd of cattle had been driven down the bank towards the last trickle of fluid, and their collapsed skeletons lay in the sand. The dented skulls lolled on their sides, each one like Quilter's, the grains of quartz glittering in the empty orbits.

33

The Train

Two miles farther on a railway bridge crossed the river. A stationary train stood among the cantilevers, the doors of the carriages open on to the line. Ransom assumed that the route ahead had been blocked, and the crew and passengers had decided to complete the journey to the coast by steamer.

They stopped in the shade below the bridge, and looked out at the endless expanse of the dry bed framed within its pillars. In the afternoon light the thousands of shadows cast by the metal refuse covered the surface with calligraphic patterns.

'We'll camp here tonight,' Philip Jordan said. 'We'll make an early start; by this time tomorrow we'll be well on the way.'

As always each evening, it took them at least two hours to prepare their camp. They pushed the cart into the shelter of one of the pillars, then drove the spears into the sand and draped the tent from the frame. Catherine and Ransom dug a deep trench around the tent, piling the warm sand into a windbreak. Philip walked up to the bank and searched the dunes for metal stakes. At night a freezing wind blew across the desert, and the few blankets they had brought with them were barely adequate to keep them warm.

By dusk they had built a semicircular embankment three

feet high around the tent and cart, held together by the pieces of metal. Inside this small burrow they sat together, cooking their meal at the fire of tinder and driftwood. The smoke wreathed upwards through the girders, drifting away into the cold night air.

While the two women prepared their meal Ransom and Philip Jordan climbed up on to the bridge. The splitting hulks of the passenger coaches sat between the cantilevers, the stars shining through the rents in their roofs. Philip began to tear armfuls of the dry wood from the sides of the coaches. Rotted suitcases and haversacks lay in the dust by the tracks. Ransom walked forward along the line to the locomotive. He climbed into the cabin and searched for a water tap among the rusted controls. Leaning his elbows on the sill of the driver's window, he looked out along the track as it crossed the bridge and wound away over the desert.

At night, as he slept, he was woken by Philip Jordan. 'Doctor! Listen!'

He felt the young man's hand on his shoulder. The glowing embers of the fire were reflected in Philip's eyes as he stared across the river. 'What is it?'

Far away to the north-west, where the dried husks of the desert merged into the foothills of the night, an animal howled wearily. Its lost cries echoed among the steel pillars of the bridge, reverberating across the white river that lay beside them, as if trying to resurrect this long-dormant skeleton of the dead land.

34

The Mannequins

At dawn the next morning they dismantled the camp and loaded their equipment into the cart. The disturbed night, and the earlier appearance of the sun each morning, delayed their departure. Philip Jordan paced around the cart as he waited for Mrs Quilter, tapping his spear restlessly against the spokes of the wheel. In the sunlight his beaked face gave him the appearance of a nervous desert nomad, scion of a dwindling aristocratic tribe.

'Did you hear the sounds?' he asked Catherine when she appeared. 'What was it – a lion or a panther?'

Catherine shook her head. She had loosened her hair, and the long tresses lifted about her head in the cool air. Unlike Philip, the sounds of the night seemed to have calmed her. 'Neither. A dog of some sort. Perhaps a wolf. It was far away.'

'Not more than five miles.' Philip climbed on to the remains of the camp and peered across the river-bed. 'We'll be on it by noon. Keep your eyes open.' He glanced sharply at Catherine, and then looked down at Ransom, who was squatting by the fire, warming his hands over the embers. 'Doctor?'

'Of course, Philip. But I shouldn't worry. After ten years they'll be more frightened of us than we are of them.'

'That's wishful thinking, doctor.' To Catherine, he added

tersely as he strode down the embankment: 'On the cliff we saw a *lion*.'

When Mrs Quilter was ready he tried to persuade her to take her seat on the cart. Although she had slept badly and was already becoming over-tired by the journey, Mrs Quilter insisted on walking for the first hour. She moved along at a snail's pace, her tiny booted feet advancing over the cracked sand like timorous mice.

Philip strode beside her, barely controlling his impatience, steering the cart with one hand. Now and then Catherine would take Mrs Quilter's arm, but she insisted on making her own way, mumbling and shaking her head.

Ransom took advantage of her slow pace to stroll away across the surface of the river. He picked among the wind-blown debris that had spilled down the bank, windmill blades and the detached doors of cars. The cold morning air refreshed him, and he was glad that Mrs Quilter was slowing the party's progress. The few minutes alone allowed him to collect the stray thoughts that had preoccupied him more and more during their advance up the river.

As he pondered on the real reasons for their journey, he had begun to sense its true inner compass. At first Ransom had assumed that he himself, like Philip Jordan and Mrs Quilter, was returning to the past, to pick up the frayed ends of his previous life, but he now felt that the white deck of the river was carrying them all in the opposite direction, forward into zones of time future where the unresolved residues of the past would appear smoothed and rounded, muffled by the detritus of time, like images in a clouded mirror. Perhaps these residues were the sole elements contained in the future, and would have the bizarre and fragmented quality of the debris through which he was now walking. None the less they would all be merged and resolved in the soft dust of the drained bed.

'Philip! Dr Ransom!' Catherine Austen had stopped some

twenty yards behind the others and was pointing down the river behind them.

A mile away, where the bridge crossed the river, the empty train was burning briskly in the sunlight, billows of smoke pouring upwards into the air. The flames moved from one coach to the next, the bright embers falling between the tracks on to the site of the camp below. Within a few minutes the entire train had been engulfed. The sky to the south was stained by the dark smoke.

Ransom walked over to the others. 'There's a signal, at least,' he said. 'If there's anyone here they'll know we've arrived.'

Philip Jordan's hand fretted on the shaft of his spear. 'It must have been the fire. Didn't you put it out, doctor?'

'Of course. I suppose an ember was blown up on to the track during the night.'

They watched the fire burn itself out among the coaches on the approach lines to the bridge. Philip Jordan paced about, then turned to Mrs Quilter and motioned her towards the cart.

Ransom took his place at the shaft. They moved off at a brisk pace, all three pushing the cart along. Over his shoulder, when they reached a bend in the river, Ransom looked back at the burning bridge. The smoke still drifted up from the train, its curtain sealing off the south behind them.

By noon they had covered a further ten miles. They stopped to prepare their midday meal. Pleased with their progress, Philip Jordan helped Mrs Quilter down from the cart and set up the awning for her, trailing it from the hull of an old lighter.

After the meal Ransom strolled away along the bank. Cloaked by the sand, the remains of a wharf straggled past the hulks of three barges. The river widened into a small harbour. Ransom climbed a wooden quay and walked past the leaning cranes through the outer streets of a small town. The façades of half-ruined buildings and warehouses marked out the buried streets. He passed a hardware store and then a small bank, its doors shattered by axe-blows. The burnt-out remains of a bus depot lay in a heap of plate glass and dulled chromium.

A bus stood in the court, its roof and sides smothered under the sand, in which the eyes of the windows were set like mirrors of an interior world. Ransom ploughed his way down the centre of the road, passing the submerged forms of abandoned cars. The succession of humps, the barest residue of identity, interrupted the smooth flow of the dunes down the street. He remembered the cars excavated from the quarry on the beach. There they had emerged intact from their ten-year burial, the scratch fenders and bright chrome mined straight from the past. By contrast, the half-covered cars in the street around him were idealized images of themselves, the essences of their own geometry, the smooth curvatures like the eddies flowing outwards from some platonic future.

Submerged by the sand, everything had been transvalued in the same way. Ransom stopped by one of the stores in the main street. The sand blowing across it had reduced the square plate glass to an elliptical window. Peering through it into the dim light, he saw a dozen faces gazing out at him with the waxy expressions of plastic mannequins. Their arms were raised in placid postures, the glacé smiles as drained as the world around them.

Abruptly, Ransom caught his breath. Among the blank faces, partly obscured by the reflections of the building behind him, was a grinning head. It swam into focus, like a congealing memory, and Ransom started as a shadow moved in the street behind him.

'Quilt——!' He watched the empty streets and pavements, trying to remember if all the foot-prints in the sand were his own. The wind passed flatly down the street and a wooden sign swung from the roof of the store opposite.

Ransom walked towards it, and then turned and hurried away through the drifting sand.

They continued their progress up the river. Pausing less frequently to rest, they pushed the cart along the baked white deck. Far behind them the embers of the burnt-out train sent their long plumes of smoke into the sky.

Then, during the mid-afternoon, when the town was five miles behind them, they looked back and saw dark billows rising from its streets. The flames raced across the roof-tops, and within ten minutes an immense pall of smoke cut off the southern horizon.

'Dr Ransom!' Philip Jordan strode over to him as he leaned against the shaft of the cart. 'Did you light a fire while you were there? You went for a walk.'

Ransom shook his head. 'I don't think so, Philip. I had some matches with me — I suppose I might have done.'

'But did you? Can't you remember?' Philip watched him, his scarred lip lifting above the broken tooth. His eagerness to blame Ransom for the fires revealed a refusal to face up to the realities of the desert, its sudden violence and imploding vacuums. Or had he, perhaps, rightly identified Ransom with just this quality of unpredictability? Catherine and Mrs Quilter stared down at Ransom as the smoke crossed the sky.

'I'm sure I didn't, Ransom said. 'Why should I?'

From then on, despite Philip's suspicions that he had started the fires — suspicions that for some obscure reason he found himself sharing — Ransom was certain they were being followed. The landscape had changed. The placid open reaches of the coastal plain, its perspectives marked by an isolated tree or silo, had vanished. Here the remains of small towns gave the alluvial beach an uneven

appearance; the wrecks of cars were parked among the
dunes by the river and along the roads approaching it.
Everywhere the shells of metal towers and chimneys rose
into the air. Even the channel of the river was more
crowded, and they wound their way past scores of derelict
craft.

They passed below the spans of the demolished road
bridge which had interrupted their drive to the coast ten
years earlier. As they stepped through the collapsed arches,
and the familiar perspectives reappeared in front of them,
Ransom remembered the solitary figure they had seen walking along the drained bed. He left the cart and went on
ahead, searching for the footsteps of this enigmatic figure.
In front of him the light was hazy and obscured, and for
a moment, as he tried to clear his eyes, he saw a sudden
glimpse of someone three hundred yards away, his back
touched by the sunlight as he moved off among the empty
basins.

35

The Smoke Fires

This image remained with him as they completed the final stages of the journey to Mount Royal. Ten days later, when they reached the western outskirts of the city, it had become for Ransom inextricably confused with all the other spectres of the landscape they had crossed. The aridity of the central plain, with its desolation and endless deserts stretching across the continent, numbed him by its extent. The unvarying desert light, the absence of all colour and the brilliant whiteness of the stony landscape made him feel that he was advancing across an immense graveyard. Above all, the lack of movement gave to even the slightest disturbance an almost hallucinatory intensity. By night, as they rested in a hollow cut into the dunes along the bank, they would hear the same unseen animal somewhere to the north-west, howling to itself at their approach. Always it was several miles away from them, its cries echoing across the desert, reflected off the isolated walls that loomed in the grey light.

By day, when they set out again, they would see the fires burning behind them. The dark plumes rose from the desert floor, marking the progress of the river bed from the south. Sometimes six or seven fires would burn simultaneously in a long line, their billows leaning against the sky.

More than half their supplies of water were now

exhausted, and the failure to find any trace of a spring or underground channel had put an end to the original purpose of the expedition. However, none of them mentioned the need to turn back for the coast, or made a serious attempt to dig for water in the sand. Backs bent against the cart, they plodded on towards the rising skyline of the city.

The reduction in their daily water ration made them uneager to talk to each other. Most of the time Mrs Quilter sat tied to the back-rest atop the cart, swaying and muttering to herself. Philip Jordan, his dust-streaked face more and more lizard-like in the heat, scanned the verges of the river, taking his spear and running on ahead whenever the others rested. Pushing away at the cart, Catherine Austen kept to herself. Only the cries of the animals at night drew any response from her.

On the night before they reached the city Ransom woke to the distant howling and saw her a hundred yards from the camp. She was walking on the dunes beyond the river's edge, the dark night wind whipping her long hair off her shoulders.

The next morning, as they knelt by the fire sipping at one of the two remaining canteens, he asked her: 'Catherine, we're almost there. What are you looking for?'

She picked up a handful of the dust and clenched it in her fist, then let the white crystals dissolve between her fingers.

Surrounded on all sides by the encroaching desert, the city had drawn in upon itself, the ridges of brick and stone running off into the sand-hills. As they neared the harbour, the burnt-out roofs rose above the warehouses by the dock-yards. Ransom looked up at the wharfs and riverside streets, waiting for any signs of movement, but the roads were deserted, canyon floors filled with sand. The buildings receded in dusty tiers, transforming Mount Royal into a prehistoric terrace city, a dead metropolis that turned its forbidding stare on them as they passed.

Beyond the outskirts of the city, the lakeside town had vanished. Dunes sloped among the ruined walls, pieces of charred timber sticking from their smooth flanks. Philip Jordan and Ransom climbed on to the bank and looked out at the causeways of rubble that stretched away like the unused foundation stones of a city still waiting to be built. Here and there the remains of a shanty leaned against a wall, or a group of buildings stood alone like a deserted fort. Half a mile away they could see the curve of the motor-bridge, and beyond it an indistinct series of earthworks that marked the remains of Hamilton.

Ransom stared out at the lake. Where there had once been open water, a sea of white dunes reached towards the horizon, their rolling crests touched by the sunlight. Ransom waited for them to move, expecting the waves to sweep across the shore. The symmetry of the dunes, their drained slopes like polished chalk, illuminated the entire landscape.

Shaking his head at the desolation, Philip Jordan muttered, 'There's no water here, Ransom. Those fires were an accident. Quilter, everyone, they're dead.'

Ransom looked back at the dark plumes lifting into the sky behind them. The nearest was only half a mile away, burning somewhere in the harbour. Below them Catherine Austen leaned against the side of the cart. Under her awning Mrs Quilter rocked like a child from side to side. Philip began to walk down to them when the harsh sounds of barking crossed the air from an isolated building a hundred yards along the bank.

Philip crouched down behind a section of metal fencing, but Ransom beckoned to him. 'Philip, come on! Those dogs are given water by someone.'

They made their way across the fence, darting from the cover of one ruined house to another. The humps of car roofs and the blackened stumps of watch-towers broke through the surface. The noise of the dogs came from the far side of the building. At either end a stairway led to the shopping level on the second floor. Ransom and Philip moved carefully up the steps to the open balcony. Drifts of dust, mingled with old cans and pieces of broken furniture, had been blown against the metal balustrade overlooking the piazza. Holding their spears they crawled across to the railing. For a moment Philip hesitated, as if frightened whom he might see below, but Ransom pulled his arm.

In the centre of the piazza, some fifty yards to their left, half a dozen dogs were attacking a group of plastic mannequins taken from one of the stores and set out on the pavement. The lean white forms leapt and snarled. They tore at the faces of the mannequins and stripped off the rags of clothing draped across their waists and shoulders. One after the other the mannequins were knocked over, their arms and legs wrenched off by the snapping mouths.

A whip-like crack came from the far end of the building. The pack turned and raced off, two of them dragging a headless mannequin. Rounding the corner of the building, they disappeared among the ruined streets, the sharp cracks of the whip driving them on.

Ransom pointed to a detached head rocking in the gutter. In the savaged face he saw again the waxy images of the figures behind the store window in the riverside town. 'A warning to travellers, Philip? Or practice for the dogs?'

They returned to Catherine and Mrs Quilter. For a few minutes they rested in the shade inside the hull of a wrecked barge. In a breaker's yard across the river was the skeleton of a large fishing trawler. Its long hull was topped by the high stern bridge which Jonas had paced like a desert Ahab, hunting for his white sea. Ransom glanced at Philip Jordan, who was staring up at the bridge, his eyes searching the empty port-holes.

Mrs Quilter sat up weakly. 'Can you see my old Quilty?' she asked. During the past few days, as they neared Mount Royal, each of them had been generous with his water rations to Mrs Quilter, as if this in some way would appease the daunting spectre of her son. Now, however, with only two canteens left and the city apparently deserted, Ransom noticed that she received barely her own ration.

'He'll be here, doctor,' she said, aware of this change of heart. 'He'll be somewhere. I can feel it.'

Ransom wiped the dust from his beard. The thinning hair was now as white as Miranda Lomax's had ever been. He watched the distant plumes of smoke rising along the course of the river. 'Perhaps he is, Mrs Quilter.'

They left the trawler and set off towards the motor-bridge. They reached the shade below the pylons half an hour later. Outside the entrance to the yacht basin the remains of Mrs Quilter's barge lay in the sunlight, a few burnt beams dimly outlining its shape. She pottered over them, stirring the charred timbers with a stick, and then let herself be lifted back into the cart.

As they ploughed through the fine dust below the fishermen's quays, Ransom noticed that from here to the white dunes of the lake the surface was composed entirely of the ground skeletons of thousands of small fish. Spurs of tiny bones and vertebrae shone in the dust at his feet. It was this coating of bone-meal which formed the brilliant reflector illuminating the lake and the surrounding desert.

They passed below the intact span of the motor-bridge. Ransom let go of the shaft. 'Philip!' he shouted. 'The house-boat!' Recognizing the rectangular outline buried in the sand, he ran ahead through the drifts.

He knelt down and brushed the flowing sand away from the windows, then peered through the scored glass as Philip Jordan clambered up beside him.

Some years earlier the cabin had been ransacked. Books were scattered about, the desk drawers pulled on to the floor; but at a glance Ransom could see that all the mementoes he had gathered together before leaving Hamilton were still within the cabin. A window on the port side was broken, and the sand poured across the deck, half-submerging the framed reproduction of Tanguy's painting, the image of drained strands. Ransom's paper-weight, the fragment of Jurassic limestone, lay just beyond the reach of the sand.

'Doctor, what about the water?' Philip Jordan knelt beside him, scooping the sand away with his hands. 'You had some water in a secret tank.'

Ransom stood up, and brushed the dust from his ragged clothes. 'Under the galley. Get in round the other side.' As Philip stepped over the roof and began to drive the sand down the slope, kicking at it with his long legs, Ransom peered through the window. The care he had given to furnishing the houseboat, the mementoes with which he had stocked it like the cargo of some psychic ark, almost convinced him that it had been prepared in the future, and then stranded on the bank ten years ahead in anticipation of his present needs.

'Over here, doctor!' Philip called. Ransom left the window and crossed the roof. Fifty yards to his right Catherine Austen was climbing the bank, gazing up at the ruins of her villa.

'Have you found it, Philip?'

Philip pointed through the window. The floor of the galley had been ripped back to the walls, revealing the rungs of a stair-well into the pontoon.

'Someone else got to it first, doctor.' Philip stood up

wearily. He rubbed his throat, leaving a white streak across his neck. He looked back down the river to the fishing trawler in the breaker's yard.

36

The Mirage

The sand shifted, pouring away around their knees.

Ransom began to climb the slope to the embankment of the bridge. His feet touched a bladed metal object, and he remembered the outboard motor he had abandoned by the houseboat. For some reason he now wanted to get away from the others. During the journey from the coast they had relied on one another, but with their arrival at Hamilton, at the very point from which they had set out ten years earlier, he felt that all his obligations to them had been discharged. As he climbed the embankment he looked down at them. Isolated from each other in the unvarying light, they were held together only by the sand pouring between their feet.

He pulled himself over the balustrade and limped along the pavement towards the centre of the span. The surface was covered with pieces of metal and old tyres. He rested on the rail, gazing out across the dune-covered ruins that surrounded the empty towers of the distant city. To the north-east the white surface of the lake rolled onwards to the horizon.

He sat down by a gap in the balustrade, surrounded by the empty cans and litter, like an exhausted mendicant. Below him Philip Jordan made his way along the river-bed, spear in hand and one of the two canteens over his shoulder. Catherine Austen was moving diagonally away from him up the bank, searching for something among the splinters of driftwood. Only Mrs Quilter still sat on the cart below her tattered awning.

For ten minutes Ransom leaned against the balustrade in the centre of the deserted bridge, watching the figures below move away.

Vaguely hoping for a glimpse of his own house, he scanned the slopes of rubble. His eye was distracted by a gleam of light. Cradled among the dunes near the site of Lomax's mansion was what appeared to be a small pond of blue water, its surface ruffled into vivid patterns. Watching it, Ransom decided that the pond was a mirage of remarkable intensity. At least a hundred feet in diameter, the water was ringed by a narrow beach of sand shaped like the banks of a miniature reservoir. The dunes and ruined walls surrounded it on all sides.

As he waited for the mirage to fade, a white bird crossed the ruins and swooped down over the water. Furling its wings, it landed on the surface, gliding along, a wake of breaking light.

Ransom climbed to his feet and hurried forward across the bridge. Giving up any attempt to find the others, he straddled the rail at the lower end and slid down the embankment. Pausing to rest every fifty yards, he ran along the water-front streets, stepping on the roofs of cars buried under the sand.

'Doctor!' As he clambered over a low wall, Ransom almost jumped on to the diminutive form of Mrs Quilter, crouching below him in a crevice. She gazed up at him with timid eyes. Somehow she had managed to dismount from the cart and make her way up the bank. 'Doctor,' she sighed plaintively, 'I can't move myself.'

When Ransom was about to run on she fished the second canteen from beneath her silks. 'I'll share it with you, doctor.'

'Come on, then.' Ransom took her arm and helped her to her feet. They hobbled along together. Once she tripped over a partly buried cable and sat panting in the dust. Ransom chafed at the delay. Finally he knelt down and hoisted her on to his back, her small hands clasped around his neck.

Surprisingly, she was as light as a child. Across the sloping dunes he was able to run for a few paces. Every fifty yards he put her down and climbed a wall to take his bearings. Sitting in one of the sand-filled swimming pools by a lean-to of burnt timber, the embers of a fire around her, she watched Ransom like an amiable crone.

As they took their final leave of the river Mrs Quilter pinched his ear.

'Doctor, look back for a minute!'

Half a mile away, below the motor-bridge, clouds of smoke rose from the houseboat, the flames burning in the shadows below the bridge. A few seconds later the cart began to burn, as if touched by an invisible torch.

'Never mind!' Tightening his grip on her legs, Ransom stumbled away across the rubble, a lunatic Sinbad bearing the old woman of the desert sea. He turned in and out of the sloping streets, avoiding the half-filled swimming pools, the dust rising behind them. Ahead he saw the ring of higher dunes that surrounded the reservoir. With a last effort he ran up the nearest slope.

He stopped when he reached the crest. Mrs Quilter slid from his shoulders and scuttled away through the refuse. Ransom walked down to the water. Stirred by the wind, a few wavelets lapped at the beach, a strip of dark sand that merged into the rubble. The lake was a small reservoir, the banks built along a convenient perimeter of ruined walls. To Ransom, however, it seemed to have dropped from the sky, a distillation of all the lost rain of a decade.

Ten feet from the water's edge he began to run, and

stumbled across the loose bricks to the firmer sand. The white bird sat in the centre, watching him circumspectly. As the water leapt around his feet the foam was as brilliant as its plumage. Kneeling in the shallow water, he bathed his head and face, then soaked his shirt, letting the cool crystal liquid run down his arms. The blue water stretched to the opposite shore, the dunes hiding all sight of the wilderness.

With a cry, the bird flew off across the surface. Ransom gazed around the bank. Then, over his shoulder, he became aware of a huge figure standing on the sand behind him.

Well over six feet tall, an immense feathered cap on its head, the figure towered above him like a grotesque idol bedecked with the unrelated possessions of an entire tribe. Its broad shoulders were covered by a loose cloak of cheetah skins. Girdled around its waist by a gold cord was a flowing caftan that had once been a Paisley dressing-gown, cut back to reveal a stout leather belt. This hitched up a pair of trousers apparently sewn from random lengths of Turkish carpeting. Their uneven progress terminated in a pair of hefty sea-boots. Clamped to them by metal braces were two stout wooden stilts nailed to sand shoes. Together they raised their owner a further two feet above the ground.

Ransom knelt in the water, watching the figure's scowling face. The expression was one of almost preposterous ferocity. The long russet hair fell to the shoulders, enclosing the face like a partly curtained exhibit in a fairground freak show. Above the notched cheekbones the feathered cap sprouted laterally into two black wings, like a Norseman's helmet. Between them a wavering appendage pointed down at Ransom.

'Quilter—!' he began, recognizing the stuffed body of the black swan. 'Quilter, I'm—'

Before he had climbed to his feet the figure was suddenly

galvanized into life, and with a shout launched itself through the air at Ransom. Knocked sideways into the water, Ransom felt the heavy knees pressing in the small of his back, strong hands forcing his shoulders into the water. A fist pounded on the back of his head. Gasping for air, Ransom had a last glimpse through the flying furs of Mrs Quilter hobbling down the bank. Her beaked face wore a stunned smile as she croaked: 'It's my Quilty boy . . . come here, lad, it's your mother come to save you . . .'

Half an hour later Ransom had partly recovered, stretched out on the beach by the cool water. As he lay half-stunned in the sunlight he was aware of Mrs Quilter jabbering away on one of the dunes a few yards from him, the silent figure of her son, like an immense cuckoo, squatting beneath his furs in the sand. The old woman, beside herself with delight at having at last found her son, was now inflicting on him a non-stop résumé of everything that had happened to her during the previous decade. To Ransom's good luck, she included a glowing account of the magnificent expedition by automobile to the coast which Ransom had arranged for her. At the mention of his name, Quilter strode down the dune to inspect Ransom, turning him over with a stilted boot. His broad dented face, with its wandering eyes set above the hollow cheeks, had changed little during the intervening years, although he seemed twice his former height and gazed about with a more self-composed air. As he listened to his mother he cocked one eye at her thoughtfully, almost as if calculating the culinary possibilities of the small bundle of elderly gristle.

Ransom climbed unsteadily to his feet and walked up the dune to them. Quilter seemed barely to notice him, almost as if Ransom had emerged half-drowned from his pool every morning of the past ten years. His huge eyes were mottled like marbled sandstone. The ambiguous watery smile had vanished, and his wide mouth was firm and thin-lipped.

'Doctor—?' Mrs Quilter broke off her monologue, surprised to see Ransom but delighted that he had been able to join them. 'I was just telling him about you, doctor. Quilty, the doctor's a rare one with cars.'

Ransom murmured, weakly brushing the damp sand from his half-dried clothes.

In a gruff voice, Quilter said: 'Don't fish into any cars here, there are people buried in them.' With a gleam of his old humour he added: 'Hole down to the door, slide them in, up with the window and that's their lot – eh?'

'Sounds a good idea,' Ransom agreed cautiously. He decided not to tell him about Philip Jordan or Catherine. As yet Quilter had given them no indication of where or how he lived.

For five minutes Quilter sat on the crest of the dune, occasionally patting his furs. His mother chattered away, touching her son tentatively with her little hands. At one point Quilter reached up to the swan's neck, dangling in front of his right eye, and pulled off the head-dress. Beneath it his scalp was bald, and the thick red hair sprang from the margins of a huge tonsure.

Then, without a word, he jumped to his feet. With a brief gesture to them he strode off on his stilts across the sand, the furs and dressing-gown lifting behind him like tattered wings.

37

The Oasis

Barely keeping up with Quilter, they followed him as he strode in and out of the dunes, his stilted sandshoes carrying him across the banks of rubble. Now and then, as Ransom helped Mrs Quilter over a ruined wall, he saw the river bank and the white bone-hills of the lake, but the pattern of the eroded streets was only a distant memory of Hamilton. Nothing moved among the ruins. In the hollows they passed the remains of small fires and the picked skeletons of birds and desert wolves left there years beforehand.

They reached a set of wrought-iron gates rooted into the sand, and Ransom recognized the half-buried perspectives of the avenue in which he had once lived. On the other side of the road the Reverend Johnstone's house had vanished below the dust carried up from the lake.

Skirting the gate, Quilter led them through an interval in the wall, then set off up the drive. The shell of Lomax's mansion was hidden among the dunes, its upper floors burned out. They passed the entrance. The cracked glass doors stood open, and the marble floor inside the hall was strewn with rubbish and rusty cans.

They rounded the house and reached the swimming pool. Here at last there were some signs of habitation. A line of screens made of tanned hide had been erected around the pool, and the eaves of a large tent rose from the deep end.

The faint smoke of a wood fire lifted from the centre of the pool. The sandy verges were littered with old cooking implements, bird traps and pieces of refrigerator cabinets, salvaged from the near-by ruins. A short distance away the wheel-less bodies of two cars sat side by side among the dunes.

A wooden stairway led down on to the floor of the swimming pool. Protected by the screens, the floor was smooth and clean, the coloured tridents and sea-horses visible among the worn tiles. Walking down the slope from the shallow end, they approached the inner walls of blankets. Quilter pushed these aside and beckoned them into the central court.

Lying on a low divan beside the fire was a woman whom Ransom, with an effort, recognized to be Miranda Lomax. Her long white hair reached to her feet, enclosing her like a threadbare shroud, and her face had the same puckish eyes and mouth. But what startled Ransom was her size. She was now as fat as a pig, with gross arms and hips, hog-like shoulders and waist. Swaddled in the fat, her small eyes gazed at Ransom from above her huge cheeks. With a pudgy hand she brushed her hair off her forehead. She was wearing, almost modishly, a black nightdress that seemed designed expressly to show off her vast corpulence.

'Quilty . . .' she began. 'Who's this?' She glanced at Quilter, who kicked off his stilts and gestured his mother to a stool by the fire. Leaving Ransom to sit down on the floor, Quilter reclined into a large fan-backed wicker chair. The bamboo scrollwork rose above his head in an arch of elaborate trellises. He reached up to the swan's neck and pulled off his hat, dumping it on to the floor.

Miranda stirred, unable to roll her girth more than an inch or two across the divan. 'Quilty, isn't this our wandering doctor? What was his name . . . ?' She nodded slowly at Mrs Quilter, and then turned her attention to Ransom again. A smile spread across her face, as if Ransom's arrival had quickened some long-dormant memory. 'Doctor, you've come all the way from the coast to see us. Quilty, your mother's arrived.'

Mrs Quilter regarded Miranda blankly with her tired eyes, either unable or unwilling to recognize her.

Quilter sat in his wicker throne. He glanced distantly at his mother, and then said to Miranda, with a quirk of humour: 'She likes cars.'

'Does she?' Miranda tittered at this. 'Well, she looks as if she's just in time for you to fix her up.' She turned her pleasant beam on Ransom. 'What about you, doctor?'

Ransom brushed his beard. Despite the strangeness of this ménage at the bottom of an empty swimming pool, he felt little sense of unease. Already he had reached the point where he could accept almost any act of violence that might occur. These sudden displacements of the desert calm were its principal integers, its acts of time. 'Cars—? I've had to make do with other forms of transport. I'm glad to see you're still here, Miranda.'

'Yes . . . I suppose you are. Have you brought any water with you?'

'Water?' Ransom repeated. 'I'm afraid we used all ours getting here.'

Miranda sighed. She looked across at Quilter. 'A pity. We're rather short of water, you know.'

'But the reservoir—' Ransom gestured in the direction of the pond. 'You seem to have the stuff lying around all over the place.'

Miranda shook her head. Her rapid attention to the topic made Ransom aware that the water might well turn out to be a mirage after all. Miranda eyed him thoughtfully, 'That reservoir, as you call it, is all we've got. Isn't it, Quilter?'

Quilter nodded, taking in Ransom in his gaze. Ransom wondered whether Quilter really remembered him, or even, for that matter, his mother. The old woman sat half-asleep on her stool, exhausted now that the long journey had ended.

Miranda smiled at Ransom. 'You see, we were rather hoping you'd brought some water with you. But if you haven't, that's just that. Tell me, doctor, why have you come here?'

Ransom paused before answering, aware that Quilter's sharp eyes were on him. Obviously they assumed that the little party was the advance guard of some official expedition from the coast, perhaps the harbinger of the end of the drought.

'Well,' he temporized, 'I know it sounds quixotic, Miranda, but I wanted to see Lomax and yourself – and Quilter, of course. Perhaps you don't understand?'

Miranda sat up. 'But I *do*. I don't know about Richard, he's rather awkward and unpredictable these days, and Quilter does look a bit fed up with you already, but *I* understand.' She patted her huge stomach, looking down with tolerant affection at its giant girth. 'If you haven't brought any water, well, things won't be quite the same, let's be honest. But you can certainly stay for a few days. Can't he, Quilter?'

Before Quilter could reply Mrs Quilter began to sway on her stool. Ransom caught her arm. 'She needs to rest,' he said. 'Can she lie down somewhere?'

Quilter carried her away to a small cubicle behind the curtains. In a few minutes he came back and handed Ransom a pail of tepid water. Although his stomach was still full of the water he had swallowed in the reservoir, Ransom made a pretence of drinking gratefully.

To Miranda he said casually: 'I take it you had us followed here?'

'We knew someone was struggling along. Not many people come up from the coast – most of them seem to get tired or disappear.' She flashed Ransom a sharp smile. 'I think they get eaten on the way – by the lions, I mean.'

Ransom nodded. 'As a matter of interest, what have you been eating? Apart from a few weary travellers, that is.'

Miranda hooted. 'Don't worry, doctor, you're much too stringy. Anyway, those days are past, aren't they, Quilty? Now we've got organized there's just about enough to eat – you'd be amazed how many cans you can find under these ruins – but to begin with it was difficult. I know you think everyone went off to the coast, but an awful lot stayed behind. After a while they thinned out.' She patted her stomach reflectively. 'Ten years is a long time.'

Above them, from the dunes by the pool, there was a sharp crackling, and the pumping sounds of a bellows being worked. A fire of sticks and oil rags began to burn, sending up a cloud of smoke. Ransom looked up at the thick black pillar, rising almost from the very ground at his feet. It was identical with all the other smoke columns that had followed them across the desert, and Ransom had the sudden feeling that he had at last arrived at his destination, despite the ambiguous nature of his reception. No one had mentioned Catherine or Philip Jordan, but he assumed that people drifted about the desert without formality, and took their chances with Quilter. Some he no doubt drowned in the pool out of habit, while others he might take back to his den.

Miranda snuffled some phlegm up one nostril. 'Whitman's here,' she said to Quilter, who was gazing at his mother's sleeping face through a crack in the screen.

There was a patter of wooden clogs from behind the curtains, and three small children ran out from another cubicle. Surprised by the fire lifting from the edge of the swimming pool, they toddled about, squeaking at their mother. Their swollen heads and puckish faces were perfect replicas of Miranda and Quilter. Each had the same brachycephalic skull, the same downward eyes and hollow cheeks. Their small necks and bodies seemed barely strong enough to carry their huge rolling heads. To Ransom they first resembled the children of the congenitally insane, but then he saw their eyes watching him. Half asleep, their pupils were full of dreams.

Quilter ignored them as they scrambled around his feet for a better view of the fire. A man's hunchbacked figure was silhouetted against the screens. There seemed no point in lighting the fire, and Ransom assumed that its significance was ritual, part of an established desert practice. Like so many defunct and forgotten rituals, it was now more frightening in its mystery than when it had served some real purpose.

Miranda watched the children scurry among the curtains. 'My infants, doctor, or the few that lived. Tell me you think they're beautiful.'

'They are,' Ransom assured her hastily. He took one of the children by the arm and felt the huge bony skull. Its eyes were illuminated by a ceaseless ripple of thoughts. 'He looks like a genius.'

Miranda nodded sagely. 'That's very right, doctor, they all are. What's still locked up inside poor old Quilter I've brought out in them.'

There was a shout from above. A one-eyed man with a crab-like walk, his left arm ending in a stump above the wrist, the other blackened by charcoal, peered down at them. His face and ragged clothes were covered with dust, as if he had been living in the wild for several months. Ransom recognized the driver of the water tanker who had taken him to the zoo. A scar on the right cheek had deepened during the previous years, twisting his face into a caricature of an angry grimace. The man was less frightening than pathetic, a scarred wreck of himself.

Addressing Quilter, he said: 'The Jonas boy and the

woman went off along the river. The lions will get them tonight.'

Quilter stared at the floor of the pool. At intervals he reached up and scratched his tonsure. His preoccupied manner suggested that he was struggling with some insoluble conundrum.

'Have they got any water?' Miranda asked.

'Not a drop,' Whitman rejoined with a sharp laugh. His twisted face, which Ransom had seen reflected over his shoulder in the store window, gazed down at him with its fierce eye. Whitman wiped his forehead with his stump, and Ransom remembered the mannequins torn to pieces by the dogs. Perhaps this was how the man took his revenge, hating even the residuum of human identity in the blurred features of the mannequins. They had stood quietly in the piazza like the drained images of the vanished people of the city. Everything around Ransom now seemed as isolated, the idealized residue of a landscape and human figures whose primitive forebears had long since gone. He wondered what Whitman would do if he knew that Ransom too had once amputated the dead – neither past nor future could change, only the mirror between them.

Whitman was about to move off when the sounds of a distant voice echoed across the dunes. A confused harangue, it was addressed to itself as much as to the world at large, and held together only by a mournful dirge-like rhythm.

Whitman scuttled about. 'Jonas!' He seemed uncertain whether to advance or flee. 'I'll catch him this time!'

Quilter stood up. He placed the swan's cap on his head.

'Quilter,' Miranda called after him. 'Take the doctor. He can have a word with Lomax, and find out what he's up to.'

Quilter remounted his stilts. They climbed out of the pool and set off past the remains of the fire burning itself out, following Whitman across the dunes. Tethered to the stump of a watch-tower in one of the hollows were the dogs. The small pack, now on leash, tugged at Whitman's hand. He crept along the low walls, peering over the rough terrain. Twenty yards behind him, towering into the air like an idol in his full regalia, came Quilter, Ransom at his heels. From somewhere ahead of them the low monotonous harangue sounded into the air.

Then, as they mounted one of the dunes, they saw the solitary figure of Jonas a hundred yards away, moving among ruins by the edge of the drained lake. His dark face raised to the sunlight, he walked with the same entranced motion, declaiming at the bone-like dust that reached across the lake to the horizon. His voice droned on, part prophecy, part lamentation. Twice Ransom caught the word 'sea'. His arms rose at each crescendo, then fell again as he disappeared from sight.

Obliquely behind him, Whitman scurried along, holding back the straining bodies of the dogs. He hesitated behind the base of a ruined tower, waiting for Jonas to emerge on to the open stretch of the lakeside road. Jonas, however, seemed reluctant to approach the lake. Whitman placed the leash in his mouth, and with his one hand began to undo the thong.

'Jonas —'

The call came softly from among the dunes out on the lake. Jonas stopped and looked around, searching for the caller. Then he saw the grotesque capped figure of Quilter behind him and the dogs jerking away from the hapless Whitman.

As the dogs rushed off in a pack the tall man came to life. Lowering his head, he raced off, his long legs carrying him away across the rubble. The dogs gained on him, snapping at his heels, and he pulled an old fishing net from around his waist and whipped it across their faces. Ten yards ahead the dogs entangled themselves around the stump of a telegraph pole and came to a halt, barking over each other as they tumbled in the dust.

Ransom watched the thin figure of the preacher disappear along the lake shore. Whitman cursed his way over to the dogs, kicking at their flanks. He stood by the edge of the lake, peering out at the dunes for any sight of the invisible caller who had warned Jonas. Quilter, meanwhile, was gazing unperturbed at the hillocks of rubble. Ransom walked over to him. 'Jonas – he's here then, Jordan's father. Is he still looking for a lost sea?'

'He's found it,' Quilter said.

'Where?'

Quilter pointed to the lake, at the chalk-like dunes. The myriads of white bones washed to the surface by the wind were speckling in the sunlight.

'This is his sea?' Ransom said as they set off. 'Why doesn't he go out on to it?'

Quilter shrugged. 'Lions there,' he said, and strode on ahead.

38

The Pavilion

A hundred yards away, across the stretch of open ground separating the Lomax swimming pool from the eastern edge of the estate, a small pavilion appeared in a hollow among the dunes, its glass and metal cornices shining in the sunlight. It had been constructed from assorted pieces of chromium and enamelled metal — the radiator grilles of cars, reflectors of electric heaters, radio cabinets and so on — fitted together with remarkable ingenuity to form what appeared at a distance to be a bejewelled temple. In the sunlight the gilded edifice gleamed among the dust and sand like a Fabergé gem.

Quilter stopped fifty yards from it. 'Lomax,' he said, by way of introduction. 'Talk to him now. Tell him if he doesn't find water soon he's going to *drown*.'

Leaving Ransom with this paradox, he walked away towards the pool.

Ransom set off across the sand. As he approached the pavilion he compared it with the crude hovels he had constructed out of the same materials at the coast. However, the even desert light and neutral sand encouraged fancy and imagination, while the damp salt-dunes had drained them.

He reached the ornamented portico and peered inside. The walls of the small ante-room were decorated with strips of curved chromium. Coloured discs of glass taken from car headlamps had been fitted into a grille and formed one continuous wall, through which the sun shone in a dozen images of itself. Another wall was constructed from the grilles of radio sets, the lines of gilded knobs forming astrological patterns.

An inner door opened. A plump scented figure darted out from the shadows and seized his arm.

'Charles, my dear boy! They said you were coming! How delightful to see you again!'

'Richard . . . !' For a moment Ransom stared at Lomax. The latter circled around him, goggling over Ransom's ragged clothes with the eyes of a delirious goldfish. Lomax was completely bald, and resembled a handsome but hairless woman. His skin had become svelte and creamy, untouched by the desert wind and sun. He wore a grey silk suit of extravagant cut, the pleated trousers like a close-fitting skirt, or the bifurcated tail of a huge fish, the embroidered jacket fitted with ruffs and rows of pearl buttons. To Ransom he resembled a grotesque pantomine dame, part amiable scoundrel and part transvestite, stranded in the middle of the desert with his pavilion of delights.

'Charles, what is it?' Lomax stood back. His eyes, above the short hooked nose, were as sharp as ever. 'Don't you remember me?' He chortled to himself, happy to prepare the way for his own retort. 'Or is that the trouble – you *do*!'

Tittering to himself, he led Ransom through the pavilion to a small court at the rear, where an ornamental garden decorated with glass and chromium blooms had been laid around the remains of a fountain.

'Well, Charles, what's going on? You've brought water with you?' He pressed Ransom into a chair, his hand holding Ransom's arm like a claw. 'God knows I've waited long enough.'

Ransom disengaged the arm. 'I'm afraid you'll have to

go on waiting, Richard. It must sound like a bad joke after all these years, but one of the reasons we came here from the coast was to look for water.'

'What?' Lomax swung on his heel. 'What on earth are you talking about? You must be out of your mind. There isn't a drop of water for a hundred miles!' With sudden irritation he drove his little fists together. 'What have you been doing all this time?'

'We haven't been doing anything,' Ransom said quietly. 'It's been all we could manage just to distil enough water to keep alive.'

Lomax nodded, controlling himself. 'I dare say. Frankly, Charles, you do look a mess. You should have stayed with me. But this drought – they said it would end in ten years. I thought that was why you came!' Lomax's voice rose again, reverberating off the tinsel walls.

'Richard, for heaven's sake . . .' Ransom tried to pacify him. 'You're all obsessed by the subject of water. There seems plenty around. As soon as I arrived I walked straight into a reservoir.'

'That?' Lomax waved a ruffed hand at him. His white woman's face was like a powdered mask. Mopping his brow with a soft hand, he noticed his bald pate, then quickly pulled a small peruke from his pocket and slipped it on to his scalp. 'That water, Charles, don't you understand – that's all there is left! For ten years I've kept them going, and now this confounded drought won't end they're turning on me!'

Lomax pulled up another chair. 'Charles, the position I'm in is impossible. Quilter is insane – have you seen him, striding about on those stilts?. . . He's out to destroy me, I know it!'

Cautiously, Ransom said: 'He did give me a message – something about drowning, if I remember. There's not much danger of that here.'

'Oh no?' Lomax snapped his fingers. 'Drowning — after all I've done for him! If it hadn't been for me they would have died within a week.'

He subsided into the chair. Surrounded by all the chromium and tinsel, he looked like a stranded carnival fish, encrusted with pearls and pieces of shell.

'Where did you find all this water?' Ransom asked.

'Here and there, Charles.' Lomax gestured vaguely. 'I happened to know about one or two stand-by reservoirs, forgotten for years under car parks and football fields, small ones no one ever thought of, but a hell of a lot of water in them all the same. I showed Quilter where they were, and he and the others piped the water in here.'

'And that reservoir is the last? But why should Quilter blame you? Surely they're grateful—'

'They're *not* grateful! You obviously don't understand how their minds work. Look what Quilter's done to my poor Miranda. Those diseased, cretinous children! Think what they'll be like if they're allowed to grow up. *Three* Quilters! Sometimes I think the Almighty keeps this drought going just to make sure they die of thirst.'

'Why don't you pack up and leave?'

'I can't! Don't you realize I'm a prisoner here? That terrible one-armed man Whitman is everywhere with his mad animals. I warn you, don't wander about on your own too much. There are a couple of lions around somewhere.'

Ransom stood up. 'What shall I tell Quilter?'

Lomax whipped off his wig and slipped it into his pocket. 'Tell them to go! I'm tired of playing Father Neptune. This is *my* water, I found it and I'm going to drink it!' With a smirk, he added: 'I'll share it with you, Charles, of course.'

'Thank you, Richard. I think I need to be on my own at present.'

'Very well, dear boy.' Lomax gazed at him coolly, the

smirk on his face puffing out his powdered cheeks. 'Don't expect any water, though. Sooner or later it's going to run out, perhaps sooner than later.'

'I dare say.' Ransom gazed down at Lomax, realizing how far he had decayed during the previous ten years. The serpent in this dusty Eden, he was now trying to grasp back his apple, and preserve intact, if only for a few weeks, the world before the drought. For Ransom, by contrast, the long journey up the river had been an expedition into his own future, into a world of volitional time where the images of the past were reflected free from the demands of memory and nostalgia, free even from the pressure of thirst and hunger.

'Charles, wait!' As Ransom reached the entrance to the pavilion Lomax hurried after him. 'Don't leave yet, you're the only one I can trust!' Lomax plucked at his sleeve. His voice sank to a plaintive whisper. 'They'll kill me, Charles, or turn me into a beast. Look what he's done to Miranda.'

Ransom shook his head. 'I don't agree, Richard,' he said. 'I think she's beautiful.'

Lomax gazed after him, apparently stunned by this remark. Ransom set off across the sand. Watching him in the distance from a dune above the swimming pool, the last smoke of the signal fire rising beside him, was the stilted figure of Quilter, the swan's head wavering against the evening sky.

39

The Androgyne

For the next week Ransom remained with Quilter and Miranda, watching the disintegration of Richard Lomax. Ransom decided that as soon as possible he would continue his journey across the drained lake, but at night he could hear the sounds of the lions baying among the dunes. The tall figure of Jonas would move along the lakeside road through the darkness, calling in his deep voice to the lions, which grumbled back at him. Their survival, confirming the fisher-captain's obsession with a lost river or lake, convinced Ransom that as soon as he had recovered he should carry on his search.

During the day he sat in the shade of the ruined loggia beside the swimming pool. In the morning he went off towards the city with Whitman and Quilter to forage for food. At intervals among the dunes deep shafts had been sunk into the basements of the sometime supermarkets. They would slide down them and crawl among the old freezer plant, mining out a few cans from the annealed sand. Most of them had perished, and the rancid contents were flung to the dogs or left among the rubble, where the few birds picked at them. Ransom was not surprised to find that Quilter's food stores consisted of barely a day's supplies, nor that he was becoming progressively less interested in replenishing them. He seemed to accept that the coming end of the water in the reservoir would commit him finally to the desert, and that the drained river would now take him on its own terms.

Quilter built a small hutch for his mother in the entrance hall of the house. She retired here in the evenings after spending the day with Miranda and the children.

Ransom slept in one of the wrecked cars near the pool. Whitman lived in the next vehicle, but after Ransom's arrival he moved off with his dogs and took up residence inside a drained fountain fifty yards from Lomax's pavilion. Keeping to himself, he would snarl and grumble whenever Ransom approached.

Quilter, however, spent much of his time wandering around the edge of the pool, almost as if he were trying to form some sort of relationship with Ransom, though unable to find a point of contact. Sometimes he would sit down in the dust a few feet from Ransom, letting the children climb over his shoulders and pull at his furs and swan's cap.

At intervals this placid domestic scene would be interrupted by the appearance of Richard Lomax. His performances, as Ransom regarded them, usually took the same form.

Shortly before noon there was a sudden commotion from the pavilion, and sound of gongs ringing from the gilded spires. Quilter listened to this impassively, drawing obscure patterns in the dust with a finger for his children to puzzle over. There was a shout and crackle as Lomax let off a firework. It fizzed away across the dunes, the bright trail dissolving crisply in the warm air. At last Lomax himself emerged, fully accoutred and pomaded, mincing out in his preposterous grey silk suit. Frowning angrily, he waved his arms, shouting insults at Quilter, and pointing repeatedly towards the reservoir. As Quilter leaned back on one elbow, Whitman crept up on Lomax with his dogs.

Lomax's tirade then mounted to a frenzied babble, his face working itself into a grotesque mask. Watching this tottering desert androgyne, Ransom could see that Lomax was reverting to a primitive level where the differentiation into male and female no longer occurred.

At last, when the children seemed frightened, Quilter signalled to Whitman and a dog was let off at Lomax. In a flash of white fur the beast hurled itself at the architect, who turned and fled, slamming the jewelled door into the dog's face.

For the rest of the day there was silence, until the performance the following morning. Although the firecrackers and grimacing had presumably been effective during the previous years in dispersing other desert nomads who stumbled upon the oasis, Quilter seemed immune.

Brooding most of the time, and aware of the coming crisis in their lives, he sat among the dunes by the pool, playing with his children, and with the birds who ventured up to his hands to collect the pieces of rancid meat. He fondled them all with a strange pity, as if he knew that this temporary calm would soon give way and was trying to free them from the need for water and food. Once or twice, as Quilter played with the birds, Ransom heard a strangled croak, and saw the crushed plumage twisting slowly in Quilter's hands. Ransom watched the children as they waddled about under their swollen heads and played with the dead birds, half-expecting Quilter to snap their necks in a sudden access of violence.

More and more Quilter treated Whitman and Ransom in the same way, switching them out of his path with a fur-topped staff. For the time being Ransom accepted these blows, as a bond between himself and the further possibilities of his life into which Quilter was leading him. Only with Miranda did Quilter retain his equable temper. The two of them would sit together in the concrete pool, as the water evaporated in the reservoir and the dunes outside drew nearer, a last Eve and Adam waiting for time's end.

Ransom saw nothing of Philip Jordan or Catherine. One morning when they climbed the dunes by the reservoir, a familiar dark-faced figure was filling a canteen by the water. Quilter barely noticed him as he strode stiffly across the wet sand on his stilts, and by the time Whitman had released the dogs Philip had vanished.

Catherine Austen never appeared, but at night they heard the lions coming nearer, crying from the dunes by the lakeside.

40

The Dead Bird

'Quilter, you obscene beast! Come here, my Caliban, show yourself to your master!'

Sitting among the metal litter by the pool, Ransom ignored the shouts from Lomax's pavilion and continued to play with the eldest of Quilter's children. The five-year-old boy was his favourite companion. A large birth-scar disfigured his right cheek and illuminated his face like a star. His eyes hovered below his swollen forehead like shy dragonflies. Each time Ransom held out his hands he touched the hand containing the stone with unerring insight. Occasionally, he would reverse his choice, picking the empty hand as if out of sympathy.

'Caliban! For the last time . . . !'

Ransom looked up. Lomax had advanced twenty yards from his pavilion, the sunlight shimmering off his silk suit. He postured among the low dunes, his small powdered face puckered like a shrivelled fig. In one hand he waved a silver-topped cane like a wand.

'Quilter . . . !' Lomax's voice rose to a shriek. Quilter had gone off somewhere, and he could see Ransom sitting among the fallen columns of the loggia, like a mendicant attached to the fringes of a tribal court.

Ransom nodded to the child. 'Go on. Which one?' The child watched him with its vivid smile, eyes wide as if about to divulge some delightful secret. It shook its head, arms held behind its back. Reluctantly Ransom opened his empty hands.

'Pretty good.' Ransom pointed at the shouting figure of Lomax. 'It looks as if your father is using the same trick. I'm afraid Mr Lomax isn't as clever as you.' He pulled a tin from his pocket and took off the lid. Inside were two pieces of dried meat. First wiping his fingers, he gave one to the child. Holding it tightly, it toddled away among the ruins.

Ransom leaned back against the column. He was debating when to leave the oasis and take his chances with the lions when a stinging blow struck his left arm above the elbow.

He looked up to find Lomax grimacing over him, silver-topped cane in one hand.

'Ransom . . . !' he hissed. 'Get out . . . !' His suit was puffed up, the lapels flaring like the gills of an angry fish. 'You're stealing my water! Get *out*!'

'Richard, for God's sake—' Ransom stood up. There was a soft clatter among the stones, and the child reappeared. In its hands it carried a small white gull, apparently dead, its wings neatly furled.

Lomax gazed down at the child, a demented Prospero examining the offspring of his violated daughter. He looked around at the dusty garbage-strewn oasis, stunned by the horror of this island infested by nightmares. Exasperated beyond all restraint, he raised his cane to strike the child. It stepped back, eyes suddenly still, and opened its hands. With a squawk the bird rose into the air and fluttered past Lomax's face.

There was a shout across the dunes. The stilted figure of Quilter came striding over the rubble a hundred yards away, furs lifting in the sunlight. Beside him Whitman was pushing along the broken figure of Jonas, the dogs tearing at the rags of his trousers.

Ignoring Ransom, Lomax spun on his white shoes and raced off across the sand. The dogs broke leash and ran after him, Quilter at their heels, the stilts carrying him in six-foot strides. Whitman fumbled with the leash, and Jonas straightened up and swung a fist at the back of his neck, felling him to the ground. Whitman scrambled to his feet, and Jonas unfurled the net from his waist and with a twist of his hands rolled Whitman into the dust.

Halfway to the pavilion Lomax turned to face the dogs. From his pockets he pulled out handfuls of fire-crackers, and hurled them down at their feet. The thunderflashes burst and flared, and the dogs broke off as Quilter charged through them.

He reached one hand towards Lomax. There was a gleam of silver in the air and a long blade appeared from the shaft of Lomax's cane. He darted forward on one foot and pierced Quilter's shoulder. Before Quilter could recover, he danced off behind the safety of the doors.

Gazing at the blood on his hand, Quilter walked back to the swimming pool, the gongs beating from the pavilion behind him. Glancing at Ransom, who was holding his child, he shouted to Whitman. The two men called the dogs together and set off along the river in pursuit of Jonas.

41

A Drowning

An hour later, when they had not returned, Ransom carried the child down into the pool.

'Doctor, do come in,' Miranda greeted him, as he pushed back the flaps of the inner courtyard. 'Have I missed another of Richard's firework displays?'

'Probably the last,' Ransom said. 'It wasn't meant to amuse.'

Miranda gestured him into a chair. In a cubicle beyond the curtain the old woman was crooning herself to sleep. Miranda sat up on one elbow. Her sleek face and giant body covered by its black negligé made her look like a large seal reclining on the floor of its pool. Each day her features seemed to be smaller, the minute mouth with its cupid's lips subsiding into the overlaying flesh, just as the objects in the river had become submerged by the enveloping sand.

'Your brother's obsessed by the water in the reservoir,' Ransom said. 'If Richard goes on provoking Quilter there may be a blood-bath.'

'Don't worry.' Miranda fanned herself with a plump hand. 'Quilter is still a child. He wouldn't hurt Richard.'

'Miranda, I've seen him crush a seagull to death in one hand.'

Miranda waved this aside. 'That's to show he understands it. It's a sign he loves the bird.'

Ransom shook his head. 'Perhaps, but it's a fierce love.'
'What love isn't?'

Ransom looked up, noticing the barely concealed question in her voice. Miranda lay on the divan, watching him with her bland eyes. She seemed unaware of the dunes and dust around her. Ransom went over to her. Taking her hands, he sat down on the divan. 'Miranda . . .' he began.

Looking at her great seal-like waist, he thought of the dead fishermen whose bodies had helped to swell its girth, drowned here in its warm seas, unnamed Jonahs reborn in the idiot-children. He remembered Quilter and the long knives in the crossed shoulder-straps under his furs, but the danger seemed to recede. The resolution of everything during his journey from the coast carried with it the equation of all emotions and relationships. Simultaneously he would become the children's father and Quilter's brother, Mrs Quilter's son and Miranda's husband. Only Lomax, the androgyne, remained isolated, mentally as he was sexually.

He watched Miranda's smile form itself, and the image of a river flowed through his mind, a clear stream that illuminated the sunlight.

'Doctor!' Mrs Quilter's frightened face poked through the tenting. 'There's water everywhere, doctor!'

Ransom pulled back the canopy. Running across the floor of the pool was a steady stream of water, pouring off the concrete verge above. The water swilled along, soaking the piles of bedding, and then ran to the fireplace in the centre where the tiles had been removed. The embers began to hiss and steam, sending up a shower of damp soot.

'Miranda, take the children!' Ransom pulled Miranda to her feet. 'The water's running out of the reservoir! I'll try to head Lomax off.'

As he climbed the stairway out of the pool Quilter and Whitman raced past, the dogs at their heels. Winding between the dunes were a dozen arms of silver water, pouring across the bleached sand from the direction of the reservoir. Ransom splashed through them, feeling the pressure of the water as it broke and spurted. Beyond the next line of dunes there was a deeper channel. Three feet wide, the water slid away among the ruined walls, sucked down by the porous earth.

Quilter flung himself along on his stilts. Whitman followed with the dogs, hunting bayonet clasped in his teeth. They splashed through the water, barely pausing to watch its progress, and then reached the embankment. Quilter shouted, and the long-legged figure of Jonas, kneeling by the water with his net, took off like a startled hare around the verges of the reservoir. The dogs bounded after him, kicking the wet sand into a damp spray.

Ransom leaned against a chimney stump. The reservoir was almost drained, the shallow pool in the centre gliding out in a last quiet wave. At four or five points around the reservoir large breaches had been cut in the bank. The edges of the damp basin were already drying in the sunlight.

Quilter stopped by the bank and gazed down at the vanishing mirror. His swan's hat hung over one ear. Absent-mindedly he pulled it off and let it fall on to the wet sand.

Ransom watched the chase around the opposite bank. Jonas was halfway around the reservoir, arms held out at his sides like wings as he raced up and down the dunes. The dogs gained on him, leaping at his back. Once he stumbled, and a dog tore the shirt from his shoulders.

Then two more figures appeared, running out of the dunes across the dogs' path, and Ransom heard the roaring of the white lions.

'Catherine.' As he shouted she was running beside the lions, driving them on with her whip. Behind her was

Philip Jordan, a canteen strapped to his back, spear in one hand. He feinted with the spear at Whitman as the dogs veered and scuttled away from the lions, scrambling frantically across the empty basin of the reservoir. Catherine and the lions ran on, disappearing across the dunes as suddenly as they had come. Still running, Philip Jordan took Jonas's arm, but the older man broke free and darted off between the dunes.

A dog crossed the empty pool, tail between its legs, and sped past Ransom. As he and Quilter turned to follow it they saw the tottering figure of Richard Lomax on the bank fifty yards away. The sounds of flight and pursuit faded, and Lomax's laughter crossed the settling air.

'Quilter, you bloody fool . . . !' he managed to get out, choking in a paroxysm of mirth. The pleated trousers of his silk suit were soaked to the knees, the ruffs of his jacket spattered with wet sand. A spade lay on the bank behind him.

Ransom looked back towards the house. Beyond the bank, where only a few minutes earlier deep streams of water had raced along, the wet channels were drained and empty. The water had sunk without trace, and the air seemed blank and without sparkle.

Quilter strode along the bank, his eyes on Lomax.

'Now, Quilter, don't get any ideas.' Lomax flashed a warning smile at Quilter, then backed away up the slope. On his left, Whitman moved along the far side of the bank to cut him off. 'Quilter!' Lomax stopped, putting on a show of dignity. 'This is my water, and I do what I choose with it!'

They cornered him among the ruins thirty yards from the reservoir. Behind him Miranda appeared with Mrs Quilter and the children. They sat down on one of the dunes to watch.

Lomax began to straighten his sleeves, pulling out the ruffs. Quilter waited ten yards from him, while Whitman crept up with the bayonet, his stump raised. Lomax side-stepped awkwardly, and then the sword-stick flashed in Whitman's face.

'Richard!'

Lomax turned at his sister's voice. Before he could recover, Whitman lunged forward and slashed the blade from his hand, then stabbed him in the midriff. With a squeal of pain, like a pig pierced by a drover, Lomax tottered backwards against a low wall. Whitman dropped the bayonet and bent down. With a shout he jerked Lomax's heels off the ground and tossed him backwards into a mine-shaft. A cloud of white talcum shot up, churned into the air by Lomax's kicking feet as he lay upside-down in the narrow shaft.

Ransom listened as the shouts became more and more muffled. For five minutes the dust continued to rise in small spurts, like the gentle boiling of a lava vent in a dormant volcano. Then the movement subsided almost completely, now and then sending up a faint spume.

Ransom started to walk back to the house. Then he noticed that neither Miranda nor the children had moved from the crest. Miranda's face wore her usual distant smile, but the children were quiet as they watched with their all-knowing eyes. Ransom looked back along the river, hoping for some sign of Philip Jordan or Catherine, but they had vanished along the bank. The lines of ruin lay quietly in the sunlight. Far away, against the horizon, he could see the rolling waves of the dunes on the lake.

He waited as Whitman approached, head bowed as he panted between his teeth, the bayonet held in his hand like a chisel. Quilter was looking down at the drained basin of the reservoir, already whitening in the sun, and at the arms of darker sand running away across the dunes.

Whitman feinted with the bayonet, put off when Ransom offered no resistance. 'Quilt—?' he called.

Quilter turned and walked back to the house. He glanced at Whitman and waved him away, his swan's hat carried in his hand by the neck. 'Leave him,' he said. For the first time since Ransom had known him his face was completely calm.

42

'Jours de Lenteur'

The birds had gone. Everywhere light and shade crept on slowly. No longer cooled by the evaporating water, the dunes around the oasis reflected the heat like banks of ash. Ransom rested in the ruined loggia beside the swimming pool. His complete surrender to Quilter had left him with a feeling almost of euphoria. The timeless world in which Quilter lived now formed his own universe, and only the shadow of the broken roof above, adjusting its length and perimeter, reminded him of the progress of the sun.

The next day, when Mrs Quilter died, Ransom helped to bury her. Miranda was too tired to come with them, but Whitman and Ransom carried the old woman on a plank over their heads. They followed Quilter to the burial ground near the city, waiting as he searched the rubble above the car-park, sinking his staff through the sand to the roofs of the cars below. Most of the vehicles were already occupied, but at last they found an empty limousine and buried Mrs Quilter in the back seat. When they had filled in the sand over the roof, the children scattered pieces of paper drawings over it.

Soon afterwards, Philip Jordan went off to search for his father. He came to the oasis to say goodbye to Ransom. Kneeling beside him, he pressed the canteen of water to his lips.

'There's a river here somewhere, doctor. Quilter says my father's already seen it. When I find him we'll go off and look for it together. Perhaps we'll see you there one day, doctor.'

When he stood up Ransom saw Catherine Austen waving to him from a dune in the distance, hands on hips. Her leather boots were covered with the chalk-like sand of the desert. As Philip rejoined her she lifted her whip and the white-flanked lions loped off by her side.

That night, when a sand-storm blew up, Ransom went down to the lake and watched the drifts whirling across the dunes. Far out towards the centre of the lake he could see the hull of the river steamer once commanded by Captain Tulloch. Standing at the helm as the waves of white sand broke across the bows, the fine spray lifting over the funnel, was the tall figure of Jonas. Shielding his face from the wind, Philip Jordan stood beside him at the rail.

The storm had subsided the next morning, and Ransom made his farewells to Quilter and Miranda. Leaving the house, he waved to the children who had followed him to the gate, and then walked down the avenue to his former home. Nothing remained except the stumps of the chimneys, but he rested here for an hour before continuing on his way.

He crossed the rubble and went down to the river, then began to walk along the widening mouth towards the lake. Smoothed by the wind, the white dunes covered the bed like motionless waves. He stepped among them, following the hollows that carried him out of sight of the shore. The sand was smooth and unmarked, gleaming with the bones of untold numbers of fish.

The height of the dunes steadily increased, and an hour later the crests were almost twenty feet above his head.

Although it was not yet noon, the sun seemed to be

receding into the sky, and the air was becoming colder. To his surprise he noticed that he no longer cast any shadow on to the sand, as if he had at last completed his journey across the margins of the inner landscape he had carried in his mind for so many years. The light failed, and the air grew darker. The dust was dull and opaque, the crystals in its surface dead and clouded. An immense pall of darkness lay over the dunes, as if the whole of the exterior world were losing its existence.

It was some time later that he failed to notice it had started to rain.